MATCHMAKING UNDER THE MISTLETOE

HOLLIE LUCKIE

AUTHOR'S NOTE

Thank you so much for picking up *Matchmaking Under The Mistletoe!* I hope you enjoy your time in Springside! This book is full of banter, spice, and all the nosey townspeople you could ask for.

While this story is meant to be fun and lighthearted, *Matchmaking Under the Mistletoe* does contain mature content that may not be suitable for all readers. For a list of content warnings, please flip to the content list at the back of the book.

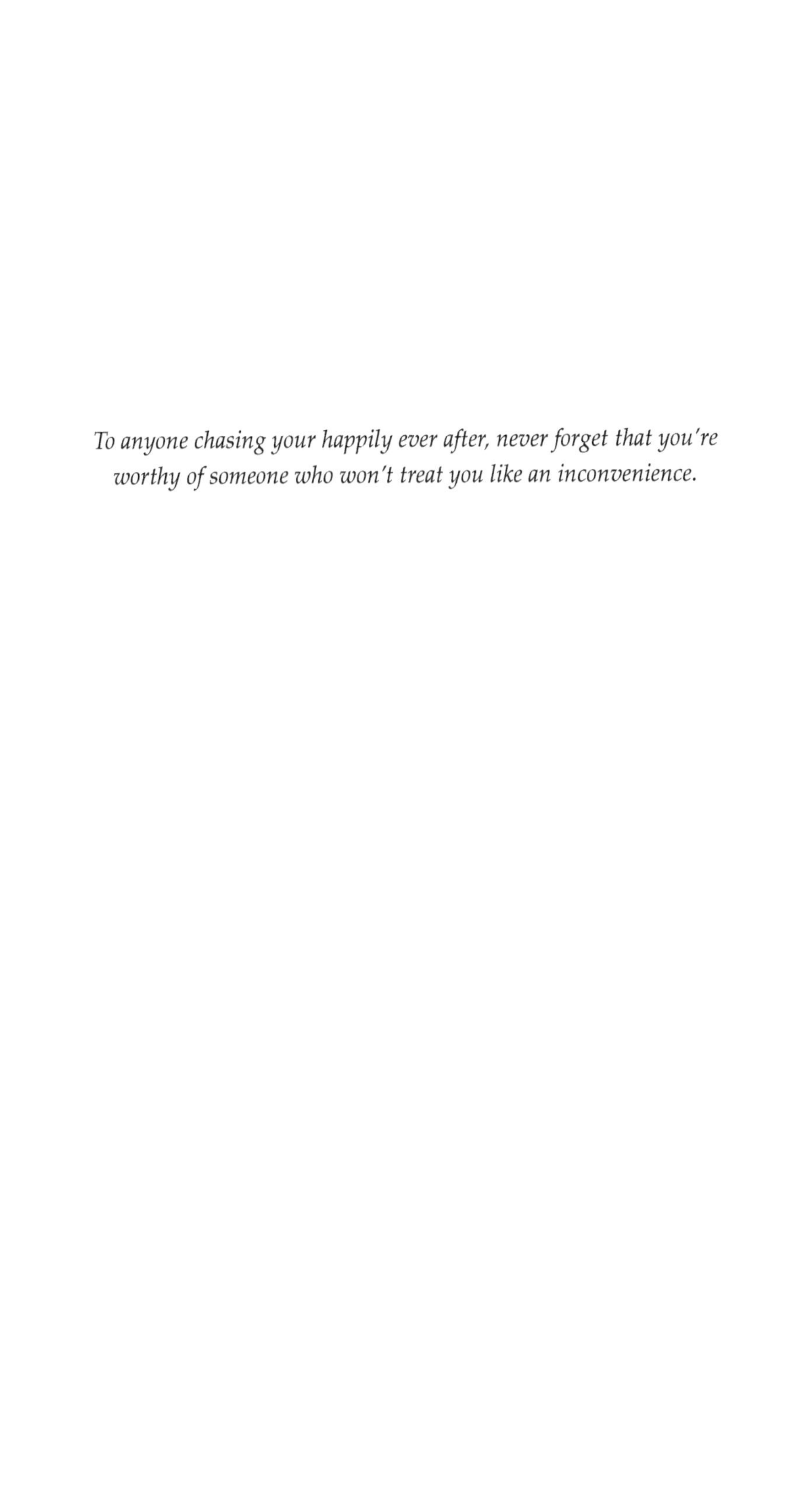

To anyone chasing your happily ever after, never forget that you're worthy of someone who won't treat you like an inconvenience.

PLAYLIST

Have Yourself A Merry Little Christmas- Kacey Musgraves
Should've Said No- Taylor Swift
Let It Snow, Let It Snow, Let It Snow- Jon Pardi
Goodbye Earl- The Chicks
I'll Be Home For Christmas- Cody Johnson
Penthouse (Healed Version)- Kelsea Ballerini
Cardigan- Taylor Swift
Run Outta Mistletoe- High Valley
We Should Be Together- Pia Mia
Christmas Tree Farm- Taylor Swift
Love Me Like You Do- Ellie Goulding
Feels Like Christmas- Brett Eldredge
Show Off- SoMo
Underneath the Tree- Kelly Clarkson

CHAPTER 1

MILLIE

know people always say the holidays are the most wonderful time of the year, but as I drive away from the life I've spent the last ten years building, I have to admit I'm not feeling too holly jolly. I'm usually all about the holiday cheer, but something about discovering my husband—or I guess as of yesterday afternoon, my now ex-husband—was sleeping with not only one, but three of his assistants, makes me start to understand why the Grinch stole Christmas.

I flip through the radio stations, trying to find something fitting for the frustration flowing through my veins, only to be met with staticky renditions of "Santa Baby" and "Rockin' Around the Christmas Tree" coming through the speakers of my old Honda Civic. Really? Where's the "Should've Said No" and "Goodbye Earl" energy when I need it? I curse myself for never pestering Allen to buy me a new car with Bluetooth over the years, but since he kept a private driver for both of us, he never saw the need.

Frustrated with the lack of options on the radio, I click the sound off and drive in silence until I hear my phone ring. Seeing my sister's name flash across the caller ID, I tap the green button to accept her call.

"Hey, sis. I just saw your text to call you. What's up? I haven't heard from you in forever. Are you okay?" my sister, Lizzie, asks without taking a breath or giving me time to answer any of her previous questions. That's Lizzie though. She's two years younger than me, and she always runs ten thousand miles a minute. I feel a pang in my chest when I think about how long it's been since I heard her voice, considering we were always close before I married Allen.

"Hey, Liz. I'm fine. Or at least physically, I guess," I say, blowing out a breath, not even sure where to start explaining all the shit that went down over the last few weeks.

"What's wrong? I swear to God if Allen the Asshole hurt you, I'll…" she starts, and I know I need to stop her or I'll never get it out.

"I found out last month he was screwing all three of his assistants," I explode and wait to see how she'll respond. The line is oddly quiet, and I'm about to check to see if my phone lost service before I hear her scream.

"HE DID WHAT? I swear to God, Mills, you have to be joking. You're joking right? What the actual hell was he thinking?" she asks, her fury palpable even through the phone.

"Definitely not kidding. I don't know what he was thinking other than being sure none of us would ever find out about the others. Obviously, they all knew he was married, but I don't blame them for falling for his act. You and I both know how charming he can be when he wants to. He told them I was leaving him. He even said I was cheating on him with the pool boy. Lizzie, we didn't even have a pool. Anyway, like I said, this one's all on him. It's not their fault I married a cheating asshole. Apparently, they realized he was sneaking around with all three of them, because they all filed sexual harassment charges against him. That's how I found out. Even his millions won't be able to get him out of this one," I mutter bitterly.

"Oh my God. That no good, cheating, man-whore! The little,

slimy prick better hope I don't ever see his greasy headed self ever again or it's game on. Wait, Mills, what the hell do you mean this happened a month ago? Why didn't you call me sooner?" my sister asks, and I don't miss the hurt in her voice.

"I'm sorry, Lizzie. I picked up my phone to call you probably a hundred times over the last month, but I just feel so stupid. It was like talking about it made it real, and I just wasn't ready to deal with it. But Allen threw his money around to ensure it was fast. He didn't even fight for me. He just walked in the door the day I found out, took one look at me, and told me he'd get the paperwork drawn up. I mean, I was leaving his ass anyway, but it was like the last ten years meant nothing to him. I guess I just needed time to process," I admit, trying to ignore the hurt in my chest at the admission.

"Mills, you're so much better than that man deserves. You better have taken every dime he's ever made. I can't believe the nerve of that..." My sister continues calling Allen every name she can think of, and I find myself smiling a bit despite all the shit that's happened over the last month.

"I know you're right. I'll be okay. I've been suspicious for the last year or so. I've barely seen the man, other than at the charity events he's had me hosting for him. I just didn't expect it to blow up like this," I admit.

"Listen, Mills, I've held back over the last few years because I wanted you to be happy, but my God, the nerve of that bastard. First, he whisks you away from me and the rest of your friends, then he doesn't let you work just to put you in charge of his social events so he can show you off like some bullshit trophy wife. And that would have been fine if it's what you wanted, but you and I both know that wasn't the case. And then he pulls this? I think the fuck not," she says angrily.

As much as I hate to admit it, she's right. I met Allen when I was a junior in college, and I fell head over heels. He was a few years older and in town for a fundraising event at the university.

He'd already started his successful real estate company, and he was recently named in *Forbes* Thirty under Thirty. Lizzie and I had just lost our mom, and I was craving security and stability after it felt like our lives had been torn apart. By our fourth date, Allen was talking about getting married, and six months after I met him I dropped out of classes to move to D.C. with him.

At first, I thought he was being sweet by telling me I didn't need to worry about working, but as the years went on, he made it clear that he believed a woman's place is at home taking care of her family. It wasn't until years later that I realized what a narcissistic, misogynistic bastard I married. But by that time, it was too late. In the span of a few months, I'd allowed him to completely alter the course of my life, and if I'm really honest, I've been floundering ever since.

"I know, I know. I still can't believe I didn't see it earlier. But as horrible as the whole thing might have been, I think it was the wake up call I needed. We may have been married on paper for the last few years, but I think it ended a long time ago. Anyway, I'm finally leaving the city now that we're done with the lawyers," I say, hoping I don't sound as defeated as I feel.

"Where are you going to go?" my sister asks curiously.

"Honestly, I have no idea. If you were in the States I'd come visit you, but even though we signed the papers last night to finalize everything, there are some details with the bank we're waiting to get worked out. Gosh, I wish Paris wasn't a ten-hour flight," I groan, honking my horn when an eighteen wheeler swaps lanes in front of me without warning.

"Gosh, tell me about it. But you know you're welcome here whenever. Once you start to get everything figured out, you have to come see me. But that doesn't answer the question of where you're heading."

"Honestly, I don't care where I end up. I just knew I had to get the hell out of D.C. If I had to spend one more day looking at that damned apartment, I was going to lose my mind. Plus, all of my so-called friends took Allen's side in the divorce, so there's nothing left there for me anymore. I packed up everything the minute we signed the papers, and I got the heck out. I just started driving south, and I spent the night in a hotel somewhere in the Carolinas. Pretty sure I'm coming through Alabama right now. I've always wanted to be by the water. Maybe I'll make it to Florida," I tell her, glancing at the GPS, trying to get a better idea of where I am.

"I understand. Just let me know where you end up. You know, I've missed you, sis. I just hate that you're hurting. I wish I had just a minute alone in a room with that son of a bitch. He would deserve every bit of what's coming to him," she fumes, and I can't help the laughter that bubbles out of me.

"Anyway, I need to focus on something else right now. How's your fancy new job? I can't believe you're working for Becky Moreau! Her gowns are incredible," I continue, trying to infuse my voice with as much enthusiasm as I can muster.

"Oh my gosh, the new job has been amazing. I was worried that working for Becky would be like a scene out of *The Devil Wears Prada*, but she and the team have been so kind and helpful. I can't believe I actually get to work on designs that will be on the runway for Fashion Week. It just doesn't even feel real," Lizzie exclaims, and relief swells in my chest that at least one of us decided to chase our dreams.

For as long as I can remember, my sister has wanted to work with a major fashion corporation. It seemed like a pretty unattainable goal when we were growing up being raised by a single mom in Atlanta, but like she always does, Lizzie found a way to make it work. She's like our mom in that way; when there was something she really wanted, there was nothing and no one that would stand in her way. She spent years developing an incredible portfolio along with a substantial social media following, which eventually led to her getting the opportunity to work for one of the biggest fashion designers in the world. I feel a pang in my chest thinking about the fact that a career is just another thing I allowed Allen to take away from me. What other thirty-one-year-old woman do you know who hasn't worked since she was in college? When I think about the last ten years after everything I've learned about my ex-husband recently, I start to feel sick to my stomach.

Lizzie is still rambling about her new job when I blink myself back into the present. One thing about Lizzie is she can talk for hours. "We have this design for next season, and oh my goodness, Millie, it's insane. It's the most beautiful purple gown and it's covered with millions of lavender jewels, and I know it sounds tacky, but my word, it's the most gorgeous thing I've ever seen. Becky told me last week that she's so impressed, and I have a real chance at being first in line for the Head of Design position whenever she decides to retire," she gushes.

"Gosh, Lizzie, I'm so damn proud of you! That's absolutely incredible," I tell her honestly, when I hear my phone beep, warning me that my phone battery is low.

"Shit, Lizzie, I'm so sorry. My phone's on ten percent, and I have no clue where my charger is. I don't want to let it go completely dead, so I need to go," I say, sighing in frustration.

"That's okay, sis. It's late here anyway. But please, let me know where you decide to stay tonight, and be safe. I'm here whenever you need me. I'll check in soon. Love you big," she says, and I hear the sincerity in her voice.

"Love you bigger," I say, feeling my spirits lift just the tiniest bit at the mantra we've used since we were kids before the line goes dead.

The car feels empty without Lizzie's loud ramblings, but I try not to let myself dwell on it for too long. I've grown accustomed to the silence since I married Allen, considering most of my time has been spent by myself.

I look around, trying to gauge where I am since I started driving without any real direction. Truth be told, my plan only went as far as hoping to find a cheap motel to spend the next few days in while I decompress. I don't have a ton of cash since I haven't exactly been the breadwinner in our marriage, but hopefully I can stretch my emergency funds for a couple weeks until the bank gets our accounts settled. As I drive, I see signs for Saddle Ridge and Springside, Alabama, and when I pull over to a small gas station to fill up, I'm taken aback by how much the temperature has dropped since I left the hotel this morning.

After my pitstop, I fiddle with the radio some more, before it starts to rain so hard I can barely see a few feet in front of me.

I didn't check the forecast before I left, so I slow down and continue to drive, hoping it will slack off. But after about thirty minutes, as it starts to get dark, the rain starts to look different. Slowly, I notice the rain is turning to snow.

"Really? Snow? In Alabama? You've gotta be shitting me!" I groan in frustration. I continue driving, hoping to make it a bit farther south before stopping.

I make it about five more miles before my little Honda starts to slide on the ice accumulating on the road and covering my windshield. I definitely didn't have a freak snowstorm in the middle of Alabama on my bingo card, but after the way my last few weeks have been going, I don't think I should be surprised that the universe is throwing me another curveball. I slow down even more, trying to remember the rules about driving on ice, but I can count on one hand the number of times I've driven in the last ten years, never mind driving during bad weather.

God, I need to get off these roads. I feel like I'm in the middle of nowhere, but maybe I can find a motel that I can stop at for the night. Deciding to pull out my phone for a quick Google search, I reach across the passenger seat where I threw it after hanging up with Lizzy, but as I do, a flash of brown catches my eye.

What the hell?

It only takes me a second to realize a deer is running in front of my car, but at that point, it's too late. Just as I grab my cell, the doe hits me at full speed, and my car jerks hard. I swerve at the impact on instinct, and all at once, my old car is spinning across the icy road. I struggle to regain control but fail, and panic rises in my chest as the car continues to spin.

I try to keep my panic under control, before finally skidding into the deep ravine on the side of the road and hitting a medium sized tree. My airbags deploy, and I wince, momentarily frozen from the impact.

I sit in shock for a minute, before getting out to check the full extent of the damage my car sustained, and immediately know I'm in trouble. Not only do I have no clue where in the hell I am, but now I have no way out. The front of the car is caved in from the collision with the deer, and the entire passenger side looks as if it would collapse if not for the support of the tree it slammed into. Honestly, after taking in the damage, it's a miracle I'm not seriously injured. Thankfully, nothing is broken, but I have no doubt I'll be sore the next few days from the impact of the air bags. I take a breath to steady myself from the adrenaline coursing through me before checking my phone. Maybe if I can figure out where I am, I can make a plan. I've barely hit the location button before my phone screen goes black telling me my battery finally went dead.

Great.

I feel my panic rising again as I try to think about the best thing to do. Snow in the South means another vehicle may not come this way for hours. If I had to guess, even with a car and a phone, all the towns in the area have basically shut down—aren't Alabamians notoriously unequipped for the snow?

I feel myself starting to spiral, so I sit back in the car and try to take a few deep breaths. *It's all going to be okay.* I remind myself. *You are a strong and independent woman, Millie. Your husband's infidelity and the loss of your mamma didn't break you. You can handle a dead phone and a little bit of snow. Just breathe.*

After sitting for a few moments, I feel a bit more like myself. I'm starting to weigh my options—sitting in the car and risking freezing to death or walking until I see someone who could at least help me charge my phone. I've just decided that the second option is probably the better bet when I see a small ATV racing through the snowy pasture across the street. Feeling a surge of hope, I start waving, praying whoever it is will take pity on me and isn't some kind of psycho serial killer. At this point, I guess I'll take my chances.

The ATV heads in my direction, and I see an older man sitting in the driver's seat. He looks nice enough, and I remind myself this is my only option to try to combat the panic rising in my chest again. As he comes closer, I notice his ATV is wrapped in battery powered Christmas lights and the front grill has a wreath zip tied to the front. All he's missing is a Santa hat to complete the look.

"Well, howdy, ma'am. I was coming to check on my cows in this storm, but it looks like you found yourself in the middle of our Winter Wonderland. My name is Huey. What exactly happened here?" he asks, and as he looks past me and registers my car, I can see the concern on his face.

"Um, I guess I had a run in with one of Rudolph's distant relatives," I joke with a wince.

"Are you okay?" he questions, looking me up and down.

"Umm, yeah. I think so," I say to the older gentleman, looking back at my car. "I'd say probably better than the deer, but it looks like he made it out just fine since he's nowhere to be found."

"I'll be damned. You're right. Do I need to see about calling an ambulance for you? It'll probably take a while in these conditions, but I'll be happy to, if you feel like you need it."

"Oh no, that's okay. Nothing some Advil and a few good nights' sleep won't fix," I tell him, trying to muster the kindest smile I can. "But it doesn't look like I'm going anywhere in this thing. Do you have the number for a tow truck that could take me into town?"

"Umm, I do. I hate to break it to you though, they're probably buried up to their eyeballs in calls, if they're even operating. It could be a day or two until they're able to get to you. And even then, that car doesn't look drivable."

"Are you serious?" I ask, feeling my panic start to rise again.

"It's okay. Why don't we see about getting you warm, huh? Then we can go from there," the man says with a kind smile.

Well, this was definitely not how I pictured starting my new life, but I guess a few days in the middle of nowhere never hurt anyone.

CHAPTER 2

MILLIE

"Thank you for the ride," I say with a weak smile to the older man who introduced himself as Huey. "My name is Millie...uh, Millie Pouncey," I say awkwardly, deciding to revert back to my maiden name for the first time in ten years.

If Huey notices my hesitancy, he doesn't acknowledge it, and I'm thankful. "Well, it's nice to meet you, Millie. I'm glad I came outside when I did. Another thirty minutes or so and you would have been a human icicle. This cold is brutal, and like I said, it doesn't look like that car of yours is going anywhere anytime soon."

I shake my head, feeling like I'm on the precipice of going into shock from everything that's happened over the last few days. I try to center myself and feel a moment of panic at his words, even though he's not telling me anything I don't already know.

What the actual hell am I going to do in this little town? I feel like I landed myself in the inside of a southern little snow globe.

"So, what brings you to our little corner of the world?" Huey asks as we ride through the fields that are completely blanketed with snow.

"Uh, well, to be honest, I'm not exactly sure what corner I'm even in. Where exactly am I?" I ask before letting out a shaky chuckle at how absurd that sounds.

"I have to say, you couldn't have picked a better place to get stuck. You're in Springside, Alabama. Where were you headed before Mother Nature changed your plans?" the older man asks with a good-natured laugh.

Crap. How the heck am I supposed to explain that I have literally no idea what I'm doing or where I'm going?

"Well, I guess you could say I might be a bit lost on that front too," I say with a weak smile as we continue to ride.

At my confession, Huey gives me a kind smile, and I feel myself relax a bit, despite the chaos I feel surrounding me.

"Well, Miss Millie, I've gotta say, I've had two great loves in my life. My late wife Alice and this town. They've both given me more joy than an old man like me deserves. And they both always had this talent for attracting the people who need them most. And something tells me Springside may be just what you're needing too," he confesses, and I feel the sincerity in his voice.

It should seem weird for him to be sharing this much of his life with someone he just met, but instead it puts me a bit more at ease. I definitely don't believe in the supposed magic of this little dot on the map but considering the fact that he saved me from certain frostbite, I just offer him a tired smile, and we ride in comfortable silence as I lose myself to my thoughts.

The weight of the last few days hits me, and I realize I'm exhausted. I tossed and turned for hours last night in the tiny roadside motel room, trying to determine where I went wrong in my marriage before finally dozing off for an hour or two. I also came to the realization how easily I lost myself in trying to be everything that Allen wanted me to be. It started slowly, just by trying to dress and act in ways that would make him happy. But somehow, before I knew it, I became a doll he put up on a shelf and only took down when he needed me to plan an event or wear a pretty dress. I don't remember the last time I did anything for fun, or just because I wanted to.

On top of everything else, I isolated myself because Allen didn't enjoy hanging out with my "silly little college friends", and he and my sister clashed mightily every time they were in the same room together. I'd been well liked in college between my sorority and campus involvement, and my sister and I used to talk everyday, even when we were both busy with school. But by the time Allen proposed, our daily chats had dwindled down to monthly check in's as I tried to keep the peace. A rush of shame rolls through me at how easy I made it for him to control me.

"Oh my goodness, are those all your cows?" I ask loudly, shaking myself from the pity party I was just throwing myself. Right in front of the ATV are more cows than I've ever seen, making their way closer to us and letting out loud *MOOOOOOOOOO*s as we come closer.

"Yep, that's them. I don't think they're too sure about this whole snow thing, but they'll get over it," Huey says, reaching out his hand to let one of them nuzzle into his palm.

"They're huge! Did you know cows were this big?" I ask in awe, cowering into the seat a bit as a large brown cow leans in and sniffs me.

Huey tries to maintain a straight face before bursting out into laughter. "Well, Miss Millie, I've lived on a farm my whole life, so yes, I did know that. But most people tend to underestimate their size. Is this your first time seeing one up close?"

"Oh, I don't know what in the hell would've given you that impression," I say as two more of the large creatures join in on trying to get my attention.

"Sorry 'bout that. They're just hungry. I know they look scary, but they're harmless as long as you don't stand behind them. Here, why don't ya give 'em something to eat?" Huey offers before reaching into the glove box and handing out a handful of pellets.

I take them from him tentatively and let out a squeal as their sandpaper tongues scoop up the feed from my hands. After I get over the fear of them trampling me, I realize they're pretty darn cute. One of the smaller animals steps forward, nuzzling her nose into my arm, and I reach up to pet her snout, her warm breath instantly calming some of my nerves from the day.

"Huh, well, I'll be damned. I reckon Miss 46 is feeling real friendly today," Huey says, gesturing at the small black animal. "Usually that one won't come anywhere near the rest of them."

I smile, as she comes closer, nuzzling her nose into my hair, making Huey and I both laugh. I continue to feed them for a few minutes, as Huey supplies me with more and more feed, until his glove box is empty.

"All right, that's enough for now. I'll be back to check on you ladies later. Miss Millie has had quite the afternoon, and I promised to get her somewhere warm," Huey calls out to the animals, while cranking the ATV up again and taking off through the snowy pasture.

If you had told me a month ago that I'd be letting a bunch of cows eat out of my hand in the middle of a field and nuzzle their cold noses into my hair, I would have laughed. But there's something about the large animals that brings a much-needed smile to my face.

The truth is, the last few years of my life have been consumed with tasks and obligations that I don't enjoy, and I don't remember the last time I let myself be present in the moment without wondering what our social circle would think about what I was doing. Sure, I never really complained about the shopping days in Georgetown and some of the other luxuries I enjoyed throughout my life with Allen. But after a while, the Pilates classes, book clubs, and society lunches grew incredibly old, especially when it seemed like they were competitions to see who could find the hottest new instructor or plan the most extravagant event.

I can imagine how insufferable most of the women from my

life in the city would be if they were in my shoes. Honestly, if I could overlook the whole being stranded in a snowstorm aspect, the simplicity is kind of nice.

We ride for another few minutes before he pulls up to a small, rustic farmhouse. Suddenly, despite how friendly Huey has been, I feel a surge of panic realizing the reality of my situation.

Oh, God, I'm alone in a strange town in the middle of bumfuck nowhere without my cell phone and my only company is an older, albeit friendly, man I just met. I'm pretty sure horror novels have started with less. How in the HELL did I get myself into this?

Once again it seems that he recognizes my stress because he pauses before we walk inside, "Do you want to call and let someone know where you are?"

"Uhhh, well actually, my phone is dead, and I haven't memorized a number since 2001," I say with a grimace. *Shit, I probably wasn't supposed to admit that either right? God, I'm a disaster.*

Huey just shakes his head before letting out another chuckle. "Well, I'll be damned, Miss Millie. You sure know how to get yourself in a pickle, huh? Okay, what about this, would it feel better if I called down to the station and let the sheriff's department know you're here? You can tell them who you are, and they'll vouch for me. You know, just to verify I'm not wanted for any violent crimes or anything like that?"

I let out a laugh before shaking my head. "Well, you know, I don't think that would hurt if you wouldn't be too offended."

"Not at all. Just give me a second and let me find my damned cell phone; it's always running away on me. I'll be right back," he says before disappearing inside. I hear him shuffling through drawers before he comes back out with an ancient looking flip phone and dials a number.

"Hey, Sheriff Mitchell. I've got a quick favor to ask of ya," he says before rolling his eyes. "Yes, Sheriff, just because I retired doesn't mean I'm blind. I see the snow... Yes, yes, I know everyone is driving like they're assholes since they've never seen snow before, but it won't take but a second… A young lady broke down here in front of my farm, and her phone is dead. Can you just reassure her she's safe and won't end up on an episode of *Criminal Minds*?"

Huey laughs again before handing out his phone to me. "Here you go. Ask him whatever you want. I'll be inside."

He closes the door behind him, and I shiver on the porch before putting his phone to my ear. "Hey, this is Millie Pouncey. Are you the county sheriff?"

"Yes, ma'am, I'm Sheriff Mitchell. I'm sorry it sounds like you're having a bit of trouble today. But all jokes aside, I've worked with Huey for the last twenty years. I can promise you, he's as harmless as can be. Honestly, if any of my girls were in your situation, I'd want them to find someone like him," the man says, and I feel myself relax a bit more as he continues.

"He was the fire chief here until he retired this summer, and he's made a bigger, more positive impact on a lot of the kids in this town than you can imagine. I would send someone out there to help y'all out, but this snowstorm has people not knowing their asses from their elbows. We're running all over the place. But anyway, Huey will help you find somewhere to stay, and I'll have someone check in on you tonight. Why don't you let me jot your name and number down, and I'll fill in the rest of the force on your situation. We'll make sure you're safe while you're here, and Huey will give you my number in case you need anything," he says, and I can hear the phone ringing in the background.

"Okay, thank you, Sheriff Mitchell. I'll be in touch. Thanks for your help," I say before listing out my information and snapping the ancient flip phone shut and opening the front door. The house is quaint but tidy, and I'm briefly hit with the feeling that this little farmhouse held ten times the love and laughs compared to the mansion I spent the last ten years living in with Allen.

"Come on in and let me grab you some coffee. Once you're

warmed up, we'll start working on a place for you to stay. But first, why don't you tell me a bit about yourself?"

I try not to grimace at that because it occurs to me that I don't have the slightest clue what to say about myself.

I don't think I fully realized until yesterday how much of myself I'd given up to fit into the mold of the pretty little perfect wife. Outside of my daily runs through the city, my hobbies and interests died pretty soon after I said "I do", but I don't think the man in front of me would really understand that even if I told him.

"Umm, well. I'm thirty-one, and I'm from Washington, D.C. I was driving through when a deer tried to attack my car, and here we are," I say with a weak grin.

"Do you have a job? Are you single? Come on, girl, you gotta give this old man more than that. Those nothing responses might work in D.C, but the people around here are some nosey sons of bitches," Huey teases.

"Umm, no job other than running my ex-husband's social calendar. I organized several of the charity functions for him too, but that's it. I guess that answers your other question too. Newly single, I suppose," I say and try to ignore the pang of sadness I feel at that statement.

"How 'newly' are we talking?" Huey asks as he raises his eyebrow in my direction.

"You weren't kidding about the nosey son of a bitch thing, were you?" I joke, making Huey laugh.

"You have no idea," he replies under his breath.

I let out a sigh before responding, "My divorce was finalized yesterday. I found out last month that my ex-husband cheated on me for the last several years with all three of his assistants. So, I guess you could say it's pretty freaking new, but at the same time, a part of me feels like I've been on my own for years."

Huey gives me a short nod and replies, "Got it. I gotta say, if he's that much of an idiot, he doesn't deserve you anyway. Why don't I make a few calls and see if we can find you a place to stay? Judging by the damage to your car, you won't be going anywhere anytime soon. Just make yourself at home, and I'll be back in a few minutes."

With that, he stands and walks back onto the porch, and I marvel at how much my plans have changed over the last hour.

CHAPTER 3

BRIAN

"Oh my gosh, Brian, I bet I've literally called your cell a hundred times this morning. I'm sorry, but we're completely swamped. Is there any way you can come help us here at the inn?" Bridget, my cousin and receptionist at Deer Valley Inn, asks as soon as I pick up my phone.

I swear my phone has been ringing nonstop since I opened my eyes this morning. I know Springside, Alabama isn't at the top of the list for snowy places in America, but sweet baby Jesus, these people are losing their fucking minds.

"Uhh, I'm not sure Bridget. I've had to reschedule the city council meeting because half of them are scared to leave the house. I was supposed to spend the morning going through bids on the expansion we're doing on City Hall, but instead I spent an hour on hold with the lady at the Emergency Management Agency. She's trying to figure out how long this storms gonna last, and I've missed three calls from the sheriff's office because, all of a sudden, no one can drive like they have any damn sense. I'm also trying to finalize next year's budget that's due on Friday. Oh, and the grocery store shelves cleared out as soon as the word 'flurry' was mentioned. You know I don't mind helping, but do you think you can get someone else to cover? It's just not a great time to try to get away," I say, grimacing as I watch yet another car skid into the curb of the sidewalk outside my office window.

"Well, let's see, we've had eight calls today about booking weddings for the summer after that article went live yesterday in *Weddings and Wine* magazine. Which would be great if they didn't ask nine thousand questions every time they called, and the snowstorm from hell hadn't decided to make its once in a decade appearance. Also, everyone has decided the snow is a reason to drink. The winery here has had a line out the door since nine this morning, and we went from having nine open rooms in the inn down to just one in the last hour. Also, none of the staff from Saddle Ridge could make the drive over, so I've been the only one in the lobby answering phones since I got here this morning. I haven't even had time to go to the bathroom, never mind eat lunch," she says, and I instantly feel guilty.

Deer Valley Inn has been in my family for generations, and after my mom passed last year, I've done everything I can to fill in the gaps and keep the place running smoothly. Apparently, all it takes is a couple inches of snow to turn those gaps into gaping holes.

"I'm sorry, Bridget. This snow has really thrown both of our days for a loop, I guess. Wait, why isn't Helen handling the wedding stuff?" I ask, referring to the middle-aged woman I hired a few months ago to oversee events.

"God, Brian, you haven't listened to any of the voicemails I've left you this morning, have you?" Bridget snaps.

"What part of everyone's losing their damn minds are you not understanding," I growl back at her.

"Yeah, yeah… Helen called the inn when she couldn't get your cell. She got a call from her dad in Texas this morning. Apparently, he broke his hip, and he's gonna need full-time care. Her lease was ending on her apartment anyway, so she decided to move back home," Bridget explains.

"Shit," I curse. "I mean, I understand. But who the hell is

gonna handle all these Christmas events that we have coming up?"

"Uh, well, that's a great question. I'd offer to help, but there's no way I can do that and take care of everything else. I guess we're gonna need to start looking for a replacement," my cousin says.

"Bridget, the first event is in ten days. God, this is a disaster," I groan.

"Yeah, pretty much. But that's gonna have to be a problem for tomorrow. Please tell me you can get over here and give me a hand. You know I wouldn't ask if I wasn't desperate."

"Give me about an hour, and I'll be there," I say, trying not to let her hear my grimace.

"Thanks. See you then," she says before hanging up the phone.

I hear my cell let out another beep, and I hit accept without looking at who's calling, figuring it's the sheriff calling me for the fourth time to inform me there's someone else on a roadway we declared impassable hours ago.

"Mayor Brian Jones, how can I help you?" I say while checking my email to see three locals have messaged wanting to know what we're going to do about the upcoming Christmas events after they heard Helen's moving. Seriously? After living in Springside for most of my life, I've gotten used to how fast news spreads in town, but sometimes it still catches me off guard. *Do they really think I'm working on that now?*

"Hey, Mayor, how ya doing?" I hear Huey, our recently retired fire chief, ask before trying to refocus myself. Huey's a bit older than me, but we've become pretty good friends because of our jobs here in town.

"Honestly, I'm feeling like if I ever see another snowflake, it'll be too soon," I reply with a groan, and I hear Huey break into a fit of laughter.

"Damn, son, I know that's right. Listen, I need a favor," he says, and I immediately feel my curiosity rise.

"Don't tell me you're stuck on the side of the road like every other damn person in this town. If so, you'll have to call Sheriff Mitchell and let him laugh at you like everybody else. I'm swamped and my event planner just quit less than two weeks away from the first Christmas event," I say, knowing Huey rarely asks for favors.

"No, no. Nothing like that. But there's a lady here who had a bad run in with a deer, and she needs somewhere to stay. Her car's a mess, and I'm almost positive it's totaled. If so, it'll probably take weeks for her insurance to get it sorted out. Y'all got any rooms available at the inn?" he asks.

"Yeah, actually we do. I just talked to Bridget and there's one left. I'll text her to hold it for you," I tell him, already typing out a message to my cousin.

"Thanks, Brian. I really appreciate it. Wait, what happened to Helen?" he asks, sounding concerned.

"Bridget just told me her dad had a bad fall, and she's moving back home to take care of him," I explain, already dreading the process of replacing her. Holding interviews and going through resumes on top of everything else I have to do before the end of the year sounds miserable.

"Oh no, I hate to hear that. But what the hell are you gonna do about all those Christmas events? You know how wild the town goes this time of year?" he questions, like I haven't lived in Springside for the entirety of my thirty-four-year existence.

"Honestly, I don't know. You have any ideas?" I snap in frustration.

"Hmm, maybe," he ponders. "Actually, the girl that just broke down, she mentioned she's spent the last decade planning events in D.C. for politicians and billionaires. I bet she could help out and at least get you through the holiday rush, since it doesn't look like she's gonna be going anywhere soon. Maybe y'all could work something out."

I pause, surprised. That definitely wasn't what I expected him to say, but I trust Huey and know he wouldn't have mentioned finding her a job if he didn't think she'd be a good fit. Plus, by the sounds of it, she's incredibly overqualified. I picture a blonde lady in her mid-fifties quizzing me on the difference in cream and eggshell linens and can already feel my blood pressure rising, but what can I say? Desperate times call for desperate measures.

Feeling like I've come to a decision, I respond with a groan. "Sure, can she start tomorrow?"

"Hold on, let me check with her," he says, and I listen as he gives her a brief rundown of the situation.

I can't hear her response, but apparently, she agrees because a minute later he says, "Yep, she sure can. We'll be there within the hour. Oh, and you have one of those fancy new phones. Bring a charger with you when you meet us at the inn," Huey says before hanging up on me.

One thing about this town is life is never boring.

BY THE TIME I SLIDE INTO THE ICY PARKING LOT OF THE INN, I'M irritable and ready to get this meetup behind me. My phone shows sixteen missed calls from the last hour on top of the eleven that I managed to answer while I made the perilous ride over to Deer Valley.

Coming by to hire some fancy, out of towner was not on my to-do list for today, and there are about a million other places I could be right now. Instead of dwelling on it, I try to remind myself that the business my family left me won't run itself as I dig out an old sock hat and cover my ears with it before bracing myself for the arctic wind waiting to pour into the cab of my truck.

I jump out and make my way as quickly as I can to the

entrance across the guest parking lot, feeling the frigid cold settle into my bones as I walk. *Jesus Christ, it's freezing.*

Relief hits my veins as I enter the cozy lobby and the warm heat from the fireplace begins to wrap around me. I glance around at all of the guests sitting on our overstuffed armchairs, playing checkers, chatting with their neighbors, and sipping from their wine glasses while watching the snow fall out the huge windows that cover the length of the wall. Despite my frustration from earlier, I feel a small smile pulling at my lips as I look out at the view of the small vineyard covered in the blanket of snow. The weather may have been a pain in my ass today, but even I have to admit it's gorgeous.

Shaking myself from my daze, I turn and walk toward the front desk, where Bridget is attempting to work through the short line of people currently waiting for help.

"Thank God, you finally made it," she says with relief. "Can you answer the phones while I handle our in-person guests? The room you texted about was our last one, so we're full for the night if anyone asks."

"Sure thing. Hopefully, we'll have more help here tomorrow, and the snow will be gone. I have a meeting as soon as Huey gets here, but I'll help out until then," I tell her as she goes back to helping the guests that called ahead get checked in.

The next thirty minutes pass quickly as I answer three more calls about potential weddings for the next year. Bridget was right; the magazine article and social media feature that *Weddings and Wine* ran on us this week was an incredible success. We've already booked double the weddings today than we had all year last year. But by the time I see Huey's truck pull into the parking lot, I'm already realizing we're gonna need a dozen more employees to handle the influx of business.

I answer another call as I wait for him and the mystery woman to make their way inside. This one is from a guest needing to cancel their reservation for tomorrow due to the road conditions, so I focus on the computer system, moving their reservation until the spring. After sending them a new confirmation, I hang up and see Huey standing in front of me.

"Hey, old man. I see you made it over okay?" I say, reaching out to shake his hand.

"Yep, sure did. Y'all are wrapped up today, huh?" Huey asks while looking around at the room full of people.

"You could say that again," I say with a groan. "Who knew a snowstorm was so good for business?"

Huey chuckles before saying, "Listen, I really appreciate you helping Millie out. I know the circumstances are a bit unusual, but I really think she'll be a great fit here."

"Sure thing. I'm glad I could help." I nod while offering him a smile. "So, where is she? You brought her with you right?"

"Of course. She stopped by the fire on the way in to warm up. She wasn't sure if you were ready to meet her," he declares, raising his hand to beckon an attractive brunette over from where she was standing by the fire. "Come on over Millie."

I don't know what I was expecting, but this gorgeous girl with long legs and big hazel eyes definitely wasn't it. She looks to be in her late twenties or early thirties, so she's not exactly the middle-aged woman I'd been picturing.

"Hey, I'm Millie. I really appreciate you agreeing to meet with me," she says timidly, reaching out her hand to shake mine.

"Umm, yeah, of course. Nice to meet you, Millie. I'm Brian Jones. I've got you a room set aside for tonight. Here's the key and everything else you'll need. You're in room 124. Now, Huey told me you're gonna be stuck here for a bit, and we're in desperate need of some event planning help here at Deer Valley Inn. Let's step back into my office and make sure it's something you're interested in, what do you say?"

She gives me a nod as her tongue dips out to lick her lips nervously. "That sounds great. Lead the way."

The three of us pile into the small office behind the lobby, and I gesture for Millie and Huey to have a seat in the plush armchairs across from the desk I'd picked out after deciding to remodel earlier this year. This office belonged to my mother for decades, but I'd needed to make it my own to help move past my grief. I still haven't gotten everything exactly how I want it, but it's nice to have a place to work away from the hustle and bustle of city hall.

"So, Millie, Huey tells me that you've got over a decade of event planning experience. What type of events do you usually work on?" I ask as I settle into my chair.

"Well, I guess you could say a bit of everything. I planned hundreds of events for my ex-husband over the last ten years in D.C. Mostly charity galas and other company events like that," she says quietly. "The events ranged from intimate gatherings to huge events with thousands on the guest list. And most of them were formal, but I'm completely flexible depending on your needs."

I nod at her as she speaks, impressed by the types of events she's organized. I'm mildly surprised at the mention of her ex-husband, given how young she looks and how long she worked for him, but that's really none of my business, so I ignore it.

"Well, Huey actually called at a great time. One of our weddings was recently featured in *Weddings and Wine*, and apparently that in combination with a good bit of social media traction, has led to a ton of interest in our venues. To be honest, we are in way over our heads with all the events we have coming up, and there are also several Christmas events later this month that we're hosting here on behalf of the city. I've tried to stay on top of everything, but between managing this place and my position as mayor, I can't do it all. So, if you're interested, we can bring you in for the next few weeks, at least to get us through the holiday rush. Then, after Christmas you can decide if you want to stay. That should give the insurance company time to work something out with your vehicle too," I finish, interested to see what she has to say.

She looks surprised by my offer, but after a moment, she smiles. "That sounds incredible. Thank you."

"Wonderful. I know you'll need somewhere to stay, so we can include room and board into your compensation. If you'll plan to meet with me in the morning, we can get the ball rolling on the Springside Christmas events we have coming soon. Now, I just need you to sign this paperwork, and you'll be good to go," I tell her as I shuffle around my desk for a new employee packet.

I pull one out and hand it to her. She fills it out quickly while Huey and I make small talk about his farm and other town gossip. As she completes the paperwork, she nibbles at her bottom lip, and I wonder how that same pink mouth would feel against mine.

Whoa. Where the fuck did that thought come from?

Huey continues yammering about the Candy Cane Carnival that one of the churches puts on each year, but I don't register anything he says as I continue to watch Millie.

After a few minutes, she signs the last of her paperwork and gives me a small smile. "Thank you, Mayor Jones. I'm really looking forward to getting started. I'll see you tomorrow."

"What? Oh yeah, that sounds good. See you then," I tell her as she breaks me from my thoughts, and she and Huey make their way toward the door.

As she walks away, I try not to notice the way her leggings hug her slim hips from the back and fight to remind myself that the paperwork she just signed made her my newest employee. I've heard too many horror stories of women being pressured into inappropriate relationships they didn't want but being too scared to do something about it out of fear of losing their jobs, and I've promised myself I would never chance putting someone in that situation. I've always prided myself in maintaining a professional relationship with everyone I employ, and Millie will be no different.

But as she turns and gives me a small wave before making her way back out into the lobby, I can't help but wonder what the hell I'm getting myself into.

CHAPTER 4

MILLIE

By the time the sun starts filtering through the large window in my room the next morning, I've worked myself into a panic over the turn of events from yesterday. I'm desperate to get to work and figure out what the heck I've gotten myself into. When Huey mentioned the prospect of a job, I couldn't really see a reason to say no. After the last few months of hell, I'm determined to be more outgoing, and saying yes to this job seemed like a good first step.

And after the meeting with Brian I felt excited, almost like I'd been given a second chance after losing so much of myself in my marriage over the last decade. Huey insisted on helping me get the single bag that we'd managed to rescue from my mangled car up to my room and made sure I had everything I needed, including a new phone charger, before heading back to his farm.

But as I spent hours tossing and turning last night, I felt my panic rise as it edged closer to sunrise. On top of that, the longer I laid there, the more my muscles started to ache after my run-in with the tree yesterday.

What the hell made me think I could do this? I haven't worked in years, and while I didn't lie when I told Brian that I have event plan-

ning experience, it's not like I did it for a job. What if he decides I'm not qualified and kicks me out? I don't have anywhere to go...

Finally, around six I push out of bed and look for something to distract me from my thoughts. Thankfully, my phone starts to ping, and I'm forced to abandon the anxiety spiral I'm feeling. I look down, seeing my sister's response to the text I sent her last night after my phone came back on.

> Me: So first of all, I'm okay. Long story short, a deer decided to attack my car in the middle of a freak snowstorm as I was coming though Alabama. So, I'll be stranded here for a while. I'm in a little town called Springside. I'll explain more when we talk, but I'm safe.

> Lizzie: WHAT THE HELL MILLIE?! ARE YOU SURE YOU'RE OKAY?!

> Lizzie: You can't just send me messages like this and expect me to be okay not getting the full story.

> Lizzie: Where are you staying? What are you going to do while you're there?

> Lizzie: MILLIE, I NEED ANSWERS.

Shaking my head at her constant text messages, I decide to have a bit of fun with the situation. Why not, right?

> Me: Well, a nice man picked me up off the side of the road...

> Me: He told me he'd make me the queen of his trailer park if I showed him my tits. Seemed like a fair trade to me? Wasn't that so nice of him?!

> Lizzie: MILLIE POUNCEY I SWEAR TO GOD.

> Lizzie: You CANNOT be serious.

Lizzie: I mean, I've seen some pretty nice trailer
parks, but the rest of it BETTER BE a joke.

Laughing at my sister's antics and knowing she won't stop until I give her more, I tap her contact and hit the call button. She answers on the first ring, and I can already hear her yelling at me before I bring the phone to my ear.

"I swear on all things holy, Millie. You may be going through a lot at the moment, but those tits better not be any part of your living situation," Lizzie screeches, and I dissolve into a fit of giggles.

"I knew that would get you wound up. I swear, I'm good. My car did get attacked by a rogue deer, and a nice older gentleman did—" I say before my sister cuts in.

"Millie! Are you okay? Were you hurt? Why didn't you call me? How are you joking about your tits and trailer parks at a time like this? Do I need to come home? I'm slammed at work, but—"

"Sis, I promise I'm fine. Just a little sore, and definitely carless for the foreseeable future. As I was saying, a nice older man did help me out. He found a local inn that had a room available and even found me a job for the next few weeks while we decide what to do with my car," I explain, knowing if I don't interrupt her, she'll ramble for hours.

"Oh God, that was fast! What type of work did he find?" she asks, and I don't miss the accusation in her voice.

Suppressing a chuckle at her suspicion, I explain. "It's actually like a dream job, Liz. I'm staying at this inn and winery, and apparently, they just got a ton of interest in their weddings. So, between that and some Christmas events they're hosting, they need an event planner. The owner offered me the job through the holidays until I decide what I want to do."

"Well, that was nice of him. What's the boss like?" my sister asks, and I try not to think about how attractive my new boss is.

"He seems nice. I met him yesterday. Apparently, he's also

the mayor here in town, so he's juggling a lot of different responsibilities. But hopefully it'll be a good fit for the next few weeks," I tell her, trying to keep my voice even. If Lizzie figures out I'm working for someone single, young, and hot I'll never hear the end of it.

"Hmm, this town has quite the hospitality. With all those titles, he must be, what, in his sixties?" she asks suspiciously.

Damn it. I'm so busted.

"Umm no. He's probably in his early thirties…" I confess, letting my voice trail off.

"OH MY GOD!" Lizzie shrieks, and I pull my phone from my ear as she continues screaming. "I knew it! You were using your 'I have a secret' voice. Is he hot?"

I open my mouth to lie, but ultimately decide there's no point. Plus, it's been years since my sister and I got to sit and gossip about boys, and I want to soak up every moment I can with her after how distant I've been over the last few years.

"You wouldn't even believe…" I admit, and I'm pretty sure my sister's scream could call rabid dogs for miles.

"You sneaky bitch! I knew it. Tell me everything," she says in delight, and I snicker at her enthusiasm.

"Well, I've told you pretty much everything I know, but he's SO attractive. Huey hinted that he's single on the ride over here. But he's technically my boss now, so I'm certain nothing will be happening between us anytime soon. Plus, the ink on my divorce papers isn't even dry yet. Three weeks ago, I was still worried about the guest list and place card designs for the Christmas auction that Allen always asks me to organize. I'm in no place to be talking to any male. My life's a big enough mess as it is," I declare with finality, like I'm trying to convince myself as much as my sister.

She lets out a loud snort at the end of my statement, making it clear I didn't convince her either. "Whatever, sis. You may have just officially left Allen this week, but you and I both know you've been alone in that marriage for years! When's the last time he made you see stars?" Lizzie asks, and I squeak at her question.

"Oh my God, stop!" I say, too embarrassed to confess she's right. I'm pretty sure Allen and I haven't even kissed outside of his charity events in the last few years, never mind any of the other fun stuff.

"YES! I knew it! Haven't you heard the best way to get over someone is to get under someone else? You should totally test that out with the sexy inn owner!"

"I don't know, Liz. I just need to focus on putting my life back together. I don't plan on seeing or sleeping with anyone anytime soon, especially not him. I've screwed up my life enough as it is!"

"Millie, what the hell do you mean?"

"Sis, I don't know if you've realized but I've spent the last ten years married to someone who just threw me away. All my supposed 'friends' were just people Allen wanted me to be close with because it helped his business deals, and they certainly didn't take my side in the divorce. I have no car, a small suitcase of clothes, and a stash of exactly two thousand dollars of emergency funds to survive off until the bank gets their shit worked out. Who knows how long that'll take with the holidays coming up. I haven't had a job in ten years. I realized yesterday that I don't know who I am or what I want anymore, and it's making me crazy! So the last thing on my mind is my boss, despite the fact that he looks like he belongs on the cover of *GQ* magazine, okay?" I explode.

Once again, my sister lets me sit in silence for a minute before responding quietly. "I love you, sis, but you've got this all wrong. Yes, your ex-husband is a bastard, but as much as I want to kill him for hurting you, I'm not sad y'all aren't together anymore. He didn't realize it at the time, but he gave you a way out. I'll be damned if you let that fucker take anything else from you. Why do you think I never called you a St. James? That asshole didn't deserve the satisfaction of claiming your last name too after the way he treated you. So, if this new job is what's gonna make you happy, go for it. Just don't rule out an office hookup with this new boss, okay?"

I'm grateful Lizzie changed the subject at the end, because as she talked I could definitely feel the tears I've refused to let fall over the last month welling up in my eyes. As much as I can see what she's saying, a part of me still feels more like a failure than ever, and I'm almost certain a random hookup isn't going to change that.

We chat for a few more minutes about Lizzie's plans for her first fashion show as I throw on a pair of black pants and an oversized cream sweater. Brian never mentioned a dress code, but even if he had, I have approximately eight outfits so this will have to do for today. All the clothes in my closet back in D.C. never really felt like me, so when I left, I only brought the things I liked. I place my phone on speaker so I can continue to listen to my sister's monologue about a set she's working on designing while I throw my hair into a messy bun and put on some makeup. Just as I'm finishing my lipstick, I glance down at the clock and realize it's time to head downstairs for work.

"Hey, sis, sorry to cut this short, but I've gotta head down-stairs. We'll talk soon?"

"Of course! I want constant updates. See if you can snap a picture of your new boss so I know what we're working with."

"Lizzie!" I exclaim. "I will absolutely not be doing that, but okay. Love ya big."

"Love you bigger, Mills. Have a good first day!" she yells before hanging up.

I make my way out of my room and down to the lobby, where Brian is sitting behind the front desk with the young girl who was there yesterday.

I have to admit I wasn't sure what to expect when Huey mentioned an inn in a town this small. I'd half expected a rundown mom and pop roadside setup, but since I didn't have any other options, I'd accepted it anyway, figuring I could make the most of whatever it was. But instead, I was blown away when we pulled up. Deer Valley Inn is beautiful. The exterior is white with black shutters on each window, and the inside is a mixture of modern and rustic styles with exposed ceiling beams and crisp white walls. On top of that, there are huge windows overlooking the small vineyard, and I notice that the fields are still covered with snow as it continues to fall.

"Oh my gosh! I thought for sure the snow would be gone by now. Have y'all ever had anything like this?" I ask as I get closer to my new boss.

"Nope. Definitely not in my lifetime at least. But anyway, did you get settled, Millie? I know you had quite the day yesterday," Brian says, standing and stepping around the front desk.

"I did. My room was very nice, thank you, Mayor Jones," I say with a timid smile.

Bridget lets out a titter of laughter at my use of his formal title. "Mayor Jones? Honey, we ain't that formal around here. Call him Brian before his head gets any bigger than it already is. The damned people in this town like to treat him like he's royalty or something. So what if he saved a puppy from a storm drain last year and volunteers with literally every organization in the city limits? Bet they won't tell you about the time he convinced the football team in high school to roll Miss Sally's yard and blamed it on the baseball boys."

We all burst out in laughter before Brian says, "Thanks for that, Bridget. I can always count on you to keep me humble. And for the record, I don't know what on earth you're talking about. But if I did, I'd say we both know Miss Sally deserved it. Anyway, by all means, Millie, please, call me Brian."

As he reaches out to shake my hand, his elbow knocks a stack of papers from the front desk, sending them flying through the air and scattering them across the floor. "Oh, no! Here let me help you!" I say, bending down and beginning to pick them up.

"Millie, you don't have to do that! It was my clumsy ass that knocked them off," he says, blushing a little as he fumbles to collect the mess off the floor.

"Brian, are you sure you're okay? What's got you acting so jumpy today?" the woman beside him asks, grinning like she's trying to hold in a giggle.

He straightens, and I hand him the stack of papers I grabbed before he gestures to the feisty woman glaring at him. "Millie, this is Bridget, my cousin. She runs everything here on the days that I have to work at City Hall. She's also a bit of a pain in my ass, but if you need anything at all, she's your girl. Bridget, this is Millie, our new event coordinator."

I give the girl a warm smile before saying, "Hey, Bridget. It's nice to meet you. I look forward to working with you."

"Oh girl, I couldn't have been more excited when Brian told me he found someone. I've been doing the best I can to fill in the gaps, but to be honest, I don't know what the hell I'm doing. I'm so relieved to have someone who understands what on earth these people are asking for. Also, we never get new young people here in town. Brian told me you got stranded here in town with the storm. How old are you? Are you single? Do you like karaoke?" she asks, reminding me of my sister as she throws her rapid-fire questions at me.

Brian rolls his eyes at his cousin before saying, "Bridget, slow down and let the girl breathe. Not everyone runs off espresso and energy drinks."

I let out a laugh before saying, "Oh, I don't mind it. I'm thirty-one. I'm newly single, and I love karaoke despite the fact that I sound like a cat being thrown in the bath."

"Perfect. I know you have a lot to get done today with Brian, but soon you and I are going out and singing the shit out of some angry girl country music. I'll get with you soon to plan a time and place."

I blink at her in surprise before muttering, "Sounds great. See ya then."

Turning back to Brian, he lets out a laugh at my expression.

"What can I say? We Jones' never meet a stranger, and Bridget's been desperate for more people our age to move back here. Anyway, are you ready for your first day here at Deer Valley?"

A large smile starts to take over my face at his words. Despite my earlier worries, I really am so excited to get started with this new chapter of my life, even if it'll probably only last for a few weeks.

"Let's do it, boss."

CHAPTER 5

BRIAN

"Okay, let's get to it," I say as we enter my office, gesturing for Millie to have a seat. "But first, how are you this morning? Did you get some rest?"

"Oh yeah, some. It took me a while to get settled after everything yesterday, but eventually I got a bit of sleep," she says with a smile.

"Totally understandable. Do you need anything?" I ask. It didn't escape my notice, when Huey showed her to her room, that everything she had fit into a single bag, which definitely didn't seem like enough.

"Oh no, you've done plenty," she says, but as she sits, I don't miss the grimace on her face.

"I don't want to hear any of that. Seriously, are you okay? Huey said you had a pretty good wreck yesterday," I ask, scanning her for injuries.

"Oh, I'm okay. Just a little sore. After this snow moves out, I'll Uber to Walmart or Target and get what I need."

"Well, I'm glad you're feeling all right, but I hate to tell you, the closest one of those is about forty miles away, and we definitely don't have Uber in Springside."

Her mouth drops in shock. "What? How do y'all do your

shopping? Or get yourselves home when you accidentally drink a whole bottle of pinot? I don't understand!"

"We take trips into Saddle Ridge every few weeks and stock up on anything that the store here in town doesn't carry. We also have a great system of designated drivers here in town for events. Speaking of which, we'll need to contact the DD's chairperson to make sure some of them will be volunteering for the Christmas events. I know you don't have a car, but if you need something just let Bridget or me know, and we'll be happy to take you wherever you need to go. We'll have to make a few trips anyway for supplies over the next few weeks," I tell her, suddenly realizing that we'll be spending most of the next few weeks together.

"Wait, rewind. I appreciate that, but I need to recap. Did you say the DD's have a chairperson? Do they have T-shirts too?" she jokes.

"Actually, yes, they do. But DD's doesn't stand for designated drivers. They're the Driving Divas. And for the T-shirts, the Christmas ones are green and say something like 'We don't have a sleigh, but we'll dash you home'," I reply, and Millie busts into a fit of giggles.

God, that's a sweet sound. I stare at her mouth, thinking about all the other sounds I could pull from those pink lips. Lips that would feel incredible kissing down...

Damn it, really? I absolutely cannot be thinking about this woman like this, no matter how beautiful she may be. Not only is she new to town and obviously not looking for a relationship, but she's also my employee.

Shaking my head, I attempt to distract myself from the inappropriate turn my thoughts just took.

Hoping she won't notice the guilty expression I'm sure is on my face right now, I continue my explanation. "It started out as a group of older ladies who took turns driving themselves home after the town events that serve alcohol. But the group just kept growing, so now they offer it to the whole community. They just draw names out of a hat to decide who's on duty, and the one chosen takes care of everyone for the night. I'm pretty sure Mrs. Darleen is the current chair."

Millie is still laughing, and I can't help but smile at her enthusiasm. I've never met anyone with a laugh as infectious as hers. In addition to being incredibly sexy, she seems like the type of woman who is determined to see the best in people.

After a few moments, she pulls herself together and bends down to grab a large notebook and pen out of her bag. Once she's settled, she says, "All right. Driving Divas, got it. Sorry about that. I'm ready when you are."

"Why don't you start by telling me a little bit about the events you've done in the past?" I say, leaning back in my chair. I'm surprised by how badly I want to know more about her.

Before I went to bed last night, I'd run a quick background check on her just to be sure she wasn't some sort of con artist. For some reason, it felt a bit like snooping, but since she came with no references, I just needed to be certain. As I'd expected, the report hadn't shown anything suspicious, but I'd been surprised to see her ex-husband was one of the wealthiest men in D.C. After that revelation, I was even more surprised that she'd decided to stay. Even if her only experience was organizing his personal events, the caliber of events she was probably used to planning meant she was probably still overqualified for anything in our little town.

"Well, like I said last night, I've done a little bit of everything over the last ten years. Formal galas, charity events, dinner parties, benefit luncheons, and corporate holiday parties—you get the idea. Are you wanting to start with the weddings or the Christmas events?" she asks.

"Why don't we start with the Christmas events since they're coming up pretty soon. Then we can talk about how we've run the weddings over the last year, and you can make any suggestions you may have to help us make them run smoother."

"Great. How many are there?"

"Two. Just so you know, the people of Springside don't do anything halfway. We organize all of the events through the inn because it's got the space, but the whole town usually comes out. Some of them are on committees to help organize too, but we'll come back to that. So, since it's the last week in November, we've got about a week and a half until the first event. It's the Midnight Mistletoe Maze."

"What?" she asks, and I fight the urge to laugh at her expression.

"The Midnight Mistletoe Maze," I say, and her face morphs into a look of further confusion.

"I'm gonna need a little more explanation on that one, I'm afraid," she says, and I finally can't hold in my laughter anymore. "Wait, are you trying to be funny?"

"Nope, you'll come to find out Springside's chaos needs no embellishment," I tell her, and she smiles. "No one really knows how it started, but it's been a Springside favorite for decades. Everyone comes here first, and we light the big Christmas tree and serve cookies with hot chocolate for the kids and a holiday sangria for the adults. After that, everyone loads up into sleighs and trolleys to make the ride over to the Coopers' Christmas Tree Farm for the maze."

Millie is writing furiously in her notebook as I speak, and I try to ignore how freaking gorgeous she is. Her brown hair is tossed into a bun, but as she writes I notice a few strands have fallen down, and I have to grip the armrest of my chair to keep me from reaching out to tuck them behind her ear.

And the way she continues to nibble on her bottom lip makes me wonder what it would be like to be the one tasting her. I'm seconds away from losing the last threads of my self-control. I have to get control of myself before I do something that definitely wouldn't be qualified as professional.

"Does it actually take place at midnight?" she asks skeptically.

"Nope. Seven p.m. It used to be later, but we moved it up

years ago because giving sugar and cocoa to kids at midnight turns out not to be the best idea. But there's two maze times— one for the kids and their parents, and another for just adults. The adults usually grab dinner from the restaurant here between the tree lighting and the second wave of trolleys while they wait."

I pause while she continues to write and wait for her to finish before going on. "Anyway, all the houses between here and the tree farm decorate and put up lights for the ride. It's usually pretty nice, and you don't have to do anything for that."

"Oh, that's nice. I used to love looking at Christmas lights," Millie says a bit wistfully.

"I bet D.C. had some really cool lights, huh?" I ask, trying to figure out if something I said is causing her to look so sad.

"Uhh, yeah, I guess. My ex-husband thought Christmas deco- rations were tacky, so we never put anything up. He said Christmas lights gave him a migraine. So, I guess after a while I just gave up on all the fun traditions…" she says, but her eyes look distant. Finally, as if just realizing she said that out loud, she gives herself a slight shake and says, "Gosh, I'm so sorry. Enough about that. Anyway, tell me more about these mazes."

"Well, the Cooper family has run the tree farm for as long as I can remember, and they plant their trees in the shape of a maze. The farm is huge, and they just alternate fields depending on which areas have the most trees that year. We'll go out and help them string lights through all of them so that people can see. And when they make it out, there's a station for the kids to write letters to Santa and some other fun activities. Oh, and throughout the maze there's lots of mistletoe."

"Obviously," she mutters. "This is insane."

Letting out another laugh at her expression, I tease. "You have no idea. We haven't even gotten to the ballet classes or the live animals for the other events."

"This place isn't real, I swear. I've never seen anything like this," she says, and I try not to chuckle again at her reaction.

"Oh, just buckle up, Miss Pouncey, because I promise, your first Christmas in Springside will be one you never forget," I tell her. I don't know where my words came from, but after the earlier sadness in her eyes when she talked about how much she used to love the season, I only hope I can make good on that promise.

CHAPTER 6

MILLIE

Oh my God.

When Brian mentioned planning some community Christmas events for him, I pictured some pictures with Santa and maybe a gingerbread decorating class. I figured in a town this small, that would be about all there was to it. But after taking notes for the last two hours while he talked about traditions, budgets, and volunteers, I'm feeling like I'm in way over my head.

"So, let's review. Our first event is next week and it's theeeeee…" he says, dragging out the word until I fill in the blank.

"Um, Midnight Mistletoe Maze," I respond, thinking back to all the quirky details I've just frantically scrawled in my notebook.

"Great! And then to finish the festivities we have…"

"The Gingerbread Gala on Christmas Eve," I say, already thinking about some fun ways to decorate for that one.

"Awesome. Listen, I know that I just threw a ton of information at you, but it's really not as bad as it sounds. A bunch of people and organizations volunteer to help out, and they all end up being a lot of fun. Once I tell them we've brought you in, they'll be busting down the door to meet you. I don't know if Huey warned you or not, but we have some amazing people in this town who also happen to be some of the nosiest people I've ever met. So just prepare yourself," Brian says as he stands from his desk.

"Let's take a break," he continues, stretching his arms out. "You want to grab some coffee from the lobby? With the snow, I figured we'd keep all the planning inside for today, but after this weather clears, we can walk the grounds for all the events, so you know what you're working with."

"Sure, that sounds great. Thank you for helping me get everything settled," I say as we make our way back to the lobby. I hadn't noticed it yesterday, but there's a small coffee bar tucked around the corner, and as we get closer, the smell of cinnamon, expresso, and brown sugar hits my nose making my mouth water.

Brian gestures to the kid working behind the bar and after making small talk about the local high school basketball team, he says, "Anyway, Jaxon, can I get a hot vanilla latte and a..." before turning to me for my order.

"Oh, I can get my own," I say with a shy smile, digging through my pocket for the cash I tucked in there this morning.

"Millie, put your money away and order your coffee," Brian says, and I don't miss the command in his voice.

"I really don't mind," I say awkwardly, not wanting him to feel obligated.

"Millie," he says, turning toward me and looking me in the eyes, "please stop arguing, and let me buy you a coffee."

"Yes s—yeah, okay. Thanks, Brian," I babble, feeling off kilter from his gaze.

Did I really almost call him sir? What the HELL is wrong with me?

Shaking myself internally, I order a caramel gingerbread latte with extra cinnamon, and Brian gestures for us to sit at one of the small bistro tables in the corner.

"I need a break from all these events for a few minutes. Why don't you tell me more about yourself? Huey didn't give me much on the phone yesterday. Where were you headed when the storm changed your plans?" he asks.

I smile awkwardly before responding. "Would you believe me if I told you I don't know? I just got in the car and started driving. I swear I'm not usually reckless or impulsive, but I needed to get out of D.C."

"You're not on the run from the police or anything are you?" he asks, raising an eyebrow at me.

I let out a little laugh at his question. "No, nothing like that. Just the ex-husband from hell."

Brian nods before asking, "Got it. Is the divorce recent?"

"According to the lawyers, earlier this week… But the truth is, I've been single for a lot longer than that."

"Oh, I'm sorry to hear that," he says, running a hand through his hair.

"It's okay. It turns out, fucking three of your employees is a pretty quick way to end a marriage," I admit, and resist the urge to slap my hand over my mouth.

What the hell is wrong with me? Why in the world did I just say that?

He opens his mouth like he wants to ask something else but doesn't want to be rude so he stops himself and nods.

Not wanting to dive any more into the dumpster fire of the last month, I change the subject. "So, Mr. Mayor, how'd you end up in politics? You're in your, what, mid-thirties? I thought all small-town mayors were in their eighties."

He lets out a low laugh and runs his hand over his beard, and I try not to stare too hard at his mouth while he talks. "Thirty-four, actually. Now that you say that, the other mayors in South Springs county are pretty old. But I don't really know to be honest with you. It definitely wasn't in my original career path, but when our last mayor had to go into the nursing home, he asked me to run. At first, I thought he was losing it, and to be honest I don't really know what he saw in me. But Mayor

Adams was a retired police officer and claimed that he'd spent the last thirty years reading people, and he knew a leader when he saw one. I still don't know what the hell that's supposed to mean, but I guess he knew something I didn't because I really love serving this town."

I feel a pang of jealousy that he feels so confident in his career and that he's found something that he enjoys as much as he does.

"Are the elections usually stressful?" I ask, and he laughs again.

It occurs to me that I almost never saw Allen laugh in the ten years that we were together. He was always so uptight and worried about making his next business deal, but Brian looks incredibly relaxed as he tells me about his job. He's spent the entire morning talking me through my new job, and hasn't once interrupted me to answer a "more important" call. Plus, the longer I sit here, the more I notice the veins in his muscular forearms and the way his mouth tips up right before he laughs.

God, does this man know how hot he is?

"I know most elected officials would say absolutely, but honestly, no," he answers, dragging me out of my daze. "Once word got out that Adams was endorsing me, everyone just went with it. This is my second term, and I've run unopposed both times."

"Oh my gosh, how old were you when you got elected?" I ask incredulously.

"Twenty-seven."

"That's wild! Have you always lived in Springside?"

"Sure have. This inn has been in my family for decades. Other than when I played football at Alabama, I've been here my whole life."

"What? You've been holding out on me, Mr. Mayor. You were a football star?"

"Well, I wouldn't call myself a star by any stretch of the imagination, but yeah, I played," he says modestly before asking, "anyway, that's enough about me. What do you like to do?"

I open my mouth to respond, but once again, I'm hit with the realization that I have no idea how to answer that question. The last ten years just feel like a nightmare, and I can't remember the last time I did something because I enjoyed it.

"Umm, I guess I'm still figuring that out," I say, trying not to let the embarrassment show in my voice.

"Hey, nothing wrong with that," he says with a reassuring smile just as the young barista brings us our coffees. I'd been expecting a cheap paper cup, but instead, the coffee is in a huge mug, and there's a gingerbread man outline made with cinnamon on top of the latte foam.

"Here y'all go. Enjoy," he says before returning back behind the counter.

"Look how cute!" I say cheerfully.

Brian smiles and says, "Cheers, Millie. Here's to a successful Christmas season at Deer Valley."

"Cheers," I reply before taking the first sip of my drink. "Oh my gosh. This coffee is incredible!"

"Not too bad for a small town, huh? We may not have any of the big chain stores around here, but as biased as I am, I wouldn't want to live anywhere else. The coffee bar is actually something we're trying out this year. One of the newest locals is opening a bakery and coffee shop this spring, so we offered to let her use this pop-up through the holidays as a trial run since we have the space," he says as I take another large sip of my drink.

"It's literally Christmas in a cup," I say with a smile. Brian chuckles and leans across the table, and I freeze when he wipes my lip with his thumb. My body heats, and I lean into him before I can stop myself.

A moment later he moves his hand back to his side and says, "Sorry, you had some foam on your lip."

"Oh, th-thank you," I stammer, feeling like my heart is going to beat out of my chest.

Oh my GOD. What the HELL is wrong with me? I'm acting like I've never talked to a man before in my life. He wasn't flirting; just trying to keep me from looking like an idiot. Why the hell did I lean into him like he wanted to kiss me? And did I just stutter? Millie, pull it together. He's your new boss, and he's just being nice.

"Sure thing. So, are you ready to get back to work?" he asks, and I notice his voice sounds funny.

Damn it, he must think I'm insane. I literally can't do anything right these days.

Determined to bring myself back to reality, I look down at my notes and start, "Uh, yeah, so I was thinking…"

CHAPTER 7

BRIAN

few hours later, I make my way to my truck after hammering out some other details for our upcoming events. When we finished our coffee break, I listened to her brainstorm ideas while giving myself a stern talking to.

What the HELL was I thinking? Did I really just caress her lip? And who the hell even says caress? She's been here less than a day, and I'm losing my mind. She's gonna think I'm some creepy boss, and she's gonna quit. Damn it, I'm an idiot.

But not only is she the sexiest woman I've ever met, I realized that she's also incredibly funny and outgoing considering the circumstances. You would think she would be emotional after ending her marriage so recently, but instead she seems like a woman who's been given a second chance at life. I minded my manners for most of the day, but her excitement over the smallest things like a Christmas latte made me want to be closer to her.

At the same time, after hearing about the reason for her recent divorce, I'm even more determined not to step too close to the line between boss and employee. It's clear that her asshole of an ex-husband used his position to manipulate the women he worked with, and I refuse to fall into the same pattern. It just figures that the first woman I've been attracted to in years is literally the definition of "off-limits".

But God, it would be nice to spend some time with her outside of work. It occurs to me that I haven't been on a date since I graduated from college. *Shit, has it really been that long?*

I think about it for a moment, realizing it's been years since I've shared anything more than a professional relationship with a woman. Almost a decade since I've been on a date, and definitely a handful of years since I've shared a bed with a woman.

Damn, I've spent the last ten years running myself ragged, trying to take care of everyone that needed me, and somehow that's translated into neglecting myself. I bet she would feel so good wrapped around my… *Shit, I can't do this.*

Just as I'm about to chew myself out again, my phone rings. I see Huey's name on the screen and hit accept on the dashboard before putting my truck in reverse carefully. The snow finally stopped falling a few hours ago, and while the sun is currently melting the icy sludge, the roads haven't completely cleared yet.

"Hello," I say as the phone connects over the speaker.

"How'd it go?" he asks, forgoing any of the formalities.

"Geee, I can't imagine what you're talking about," I say sarcastically.

"You know darn tootin' well what I'm talking about!" Huey exclaims, causing me to chuckle. "How was her first day?"

"Pretty good, I guess," I reply, not really knowing how to answer that.

"What do you mean, 'you guess'? Did you not help her get settled today?"

"Yeah, I did. I mean, she looked pretty nervous at times, but from the sounds of it, she's had a rough couple of days, so I think that's understandable."

"Yeah, you're right about that. You think she's gonna stay?" the older man asks, concern obvious in his voice. To some it may seem strange that Huey's this concerned about someone he just met yesterday, but for as long as I can remember, he's made it his mission to take care of everyone he meets.

"Well, she didn't run screaming when I went over everything, but the snow has kept most of the locals away. To be honest, that part has me a bit concerned. We both know Springside isn't exactly gentle with new arrivals, and I get the impression Millie doesn't like talking about herself," I admit.

"I mean, I love the people of this town, but when word gets out, we both know they'll be like a dog to a bone. They're gonna go crazy over her. Remember earlier this year when the new fire chief moved in? They've barely gotten over that one, and he's already engaged," I continue, suddenly worried about the shitshow that'll be.

"Son, you ought to know better. You know that Sheriff Mitchell's wife can't hold water. He told her about Millie as soon as we got off the phone yesterday, and it hit the STS within the hour. As soon as the ice is gone, I'm afraid Deer Valley will be overrun with old ladies wanting to know her life story."

Letting out a groan, I run my hand over my face. "Great," I say without any enthusiasm. The STS stands for "Small Talk of Springside", and while it started out as a prayer request group chain for one of the local Sunday School classes, over the years it's morphed into a town-wide gossip email.

"Hell, if Miss Sally gets a hold of her, she'll be out of here, car or no car," I groan, referring to the town's biggest busybody. She's infamous in Springside for verbally attacking the town's newcomers, and I don't think I've ever seen her say anything nice to anyone. All of us locals know how to put her in her place, but while I'm sure Millie can take care of herself, my stomach churns at the thought of Miss Sally using her usual antics.

"Well, I say we stall 'em for as long as possible. I'm sure Millie needs some stuff from Saddle Ridge. The girl barely had anything in that little bag of hers. I'm sure there's some things y'all will need for the maze next week. Why don't y'all get out of town tomorrow, and I'll try to hold off some of the most eager nosey Nellie's," Huey suggests.

"Yeah, I guess you're right," I say, as I pull into the driveway of my house. "I forgot to get her cell number today though. Could you send it over?"

"Sure thing. Listen, Brian, I'm not trying to overstep. I just think that girl needs this town more than she knows. You know, it might need her too. But what the hell do I know? I'm just an old man with too much free time on my hands."

I open my mouth to say something, but my retort dies on my lips. Aside from his joke about his age, I think he might be right.

We talk for a few more minutes about various people in town, before agreeing to meet for dinner one day soon. Huey took me under his wing during my first term as mayor when he was still leading the fire station, and our monthly dinners have become a routine part of my life over the last seven years.

When I click to end the call, I put in the number Huey just sent me and type out a text to Millie.

> Me: Hey, it's Brian. I hope you don't mind, but Huey gave me your number. Would you be up for a ride to Saddle Ridge with me in the morning for some supplies?

> Millie: Oh hi! Yes, that works for me. What time?

> Me: Let's plan for 8. I'll pick you up at the inn.

> Millie: Sounds good. See you then.

Leaning back in my seat, I blow out a breath realizing I just volunteered to spend the entire day tomorrow with my very off-limits employee. Great. I guess there's no time like the present to test my self-control.

THE NEXT MORNING, THE SNOW ON MY DRIVE OVER TO DEER VALLEY has almost completely melted, and the sun has already started warming the brisk South Alabama air. I'm about to pull into one of the parking spots to wait for Millie, when I notice her huddled outside by the door. Pulling over to her, I unlock the door and wait for her to get in.

"Good morning! I hope you haven't been out here too long. You didn't have to wait outside. It's still so cold out," I say as soon as she settles into my passenger seat.

"Good morning. And it's no problem. As wonderful as the inn is, I was starting to get a little stir crazy," she says before handing over a coffee cup to me. "I went back for another latte and thought you might need a little caffeine, so this one's for you."

I smile at the gesture and take the cup from her. "Thanks. I didn't have time for coffee this morning, so I appreciate it."

Putting the cup to my lips and taking a sip, I try to hide my grimace. "Let me guess—caramel gingerbread latte?"

"Of course! With extra cinnamon. I literally dreamed about this coffee last night," she says with a moan.

I smile at her before forcing myself to take another sip. *God, I freaking hate cinnamon.* But as Millie does a happy dance in her seat over the drink, I can't bear to break it to her that I think this is possibly the worst thing I've ever tasted.

"I figured we could get some of the decorations we'll need for the event next week and there are a few other stores close by where you can grab any of the necessities you may need. Does that sound okay?" I ask, taking yet another sip of the coffee from hell.

"Yeah, that sounds great if you're sure we have time. The bag I could get to in my car only had leggings and sweatshirts. I've already worn the nicest things I have, so I need to grab a few more outfits while we're there."

"Sure thing. I don't have anywhere to be," I say, ignoring the fact that I had to reschedule three meetings this morning. But I couldn't risk the vultures descending on Millie and running her off while I was meeting with Mrs. Norma about the annual rodeo event we hold each spring.

Millie gives me another smile and sits her coffee in the cupholder between us. Her hand hovers next to it as we ride in silence, and suddenly I have to resist the urge to reach across and touch her hand.

God, there's seriously something wrong with me. Is my brain not getting the message that since she's my employee she's also incredibly off-limits?

"Oh my gosh, turn it up! I love this song!" she exclaims, pulling me from my thoughts. I look at the radio of my truck where I see "All I Want for Christmas" by Mariah Carey playing on the radio and bump the button on the steering wheel to turn it up.

I can't help but smile as Millie sings to the radio and dances in her seat. Fuck, she's so damn beautiful. If I've learned anything about her over the short amount of time we've spent together, it's that she seems determined to make the most out of every moment, which is even more impressive after the shit she's been through over the last few months. Her excitement for life is contagious. And if I'm really honest with myself, the more time I spend with her, the more I want to be another reason she can't stop smiling.

I let myself think for a moment about what it would feel like to lean over and kiss her pouty lips, but before I can get too lost in the fantasy, Millie hits a particularly off-key note, and I can't hold in my laughter anymore.

"Are you sure you want to go through with singing karaoke next week with Bridget? Between the two of you, everyone in the room is gonna be wishing they could turn the volume off on their hearing aids like Mr. Bruce does when Mrs. Ellen tells him he needs to quit smoking," I tease, and Millie lets out a loud laugh.

Yesterday, I was attracted to her. Today, seeing her like this makes me feel a desperation to have her that I've never felt before. And as I remind myself of all the reasons I can't have her, a part of me questions if it's enough to keep me from her.

CHAPTER 8

MILLIE

I know it's only three in the afternoon, but I am ready for a nap. I'm pretty sure Brian and I have visited every store in the city of Saddle Ridge gathering up supplies we'll need to decorate for the upcoming events. I also spent an hour in the cutest local boutique looking for a few more outfits. My emergency funds might have taken a hit, but the pretty dresses and neutral sweaters made me smile when I tried them on.

I've just finished piling the last of my bags in the backseat of Brian's truck and am getting settled in for the ride back to Springside when Brian's phone rings.

"Hey, Bridget, what's up?" he asks, pulling out of the parking lot before slamming on the breaks. "What? What do you mean?"

I begin to feel uneasy as I watch Brian talk to his cousin. It's clear something isn't right.

"Bridget, we're still completely full. This can't be happening. How bad's the damage?" he asks as he listens to her response on the other end of the line.

"Okay. Do you know who's in the rooms that are affected?" he asks with a groan.

"Bridget, you're shitting me. You have to be making this up.

Okay, fine, I'll figure it out. Thanks," he says before furiously tapping the end call button.

We're still sitting in the parking lot, and I wait a moment to determine if I should ask him what's going on. *Is that too nosey? I don't want him to think—*

"Well, this is just great," Brian says, interrupting my internal debate. "Bridget said that one of the pipes burst this morning from all the cold weather we've been having. They caught it in time, so it didn't flood the whole floor. She said they're working on getting it fixed, but apparently your room is uninhabitable for the next few weeks."

"Uhh, oh my. Well, that's less than ideal, I guess," I say, feeling the anxiety knotting in my chest.

God, I should have known this whole setup was too good to be true. He's gonna tell me this isn't gonna work out and I'll be on my own again.

"Yeah, you're right about that. She did say she was able to grab most of your stuff out, but they've gotta close the room off until after the insurance adjuster can come by. Normally, this wouldn't be too big of a deal, but thanks to the snow and the holidays coming up, we're completely booked, and he may not be here for a few days, on top of the time it'll take to get the damages fixed," he explains, and I feel my anxiety continue to rise.

"I don't suppose there are any other hotels in town, huh? Or an Airbnb? A bed and breakfast? A really nice lady with an air mattress? I swear, I'm not picky," I ask, feeling like I already know the answer despite the desperation creeping into my voice.

"You'd be correct on the hotel and Airbnb front. The closest chain hotel is back in Saddle Ridge. Let me think…" he says, turning onto the main road and heading for Springside. "I'll call Huey and see if he has any ideas."

He punches his phone again before holding it up to his ear. Several minutes pass before he hangs up. "He didn't answer either. Let me try Miss Sally. She's not my favorite person, but she hears everything in town. Maybe she'll know of someone I'm forgetting with a guest house or something."

He waits with the phone up to his ear for another minute before groaning. "Unbelievable. I swear, as many times as she's blown my phone up with a complaint about the grass needing to be cut at City Hall or her trash not being picked up on a holiday, but now that she could be helpful, she can't bother to answer," he says, rubbing his hand over his face.

We ride quietly for another moment before he says, "I'm sorry, Millie, this is unbelievable."

I rub my hands up and down my arms, trying not to look as uncomfortable as I feel. "Oh, it's okay. It's not your fault. I can figure something out. Maybe I can find something in Saddle Ridge until my car gets fixed. I mean, obviously I wouldn't be able to work at the inn, but—"

"Stay with me," Brian interrupts, and I feel my eyes widen. Did he just say what I think he said?

I look over at him, and for a moment he looks shocked that the words came out of his mouth before he nods reassuringly and says, "Yeah, that could work. I have a guest room and plenty of space. I mean, I know it's not ideal, and I'm not trying to make you uncomfortable. But, Millie, you can't leave. Not unless you want to, and hopefully your room will be available again soon."

I try to ignore the way my heartbeat has quickened in my chest at his suggestion, but even I have to admit our options are pretty limited. And despite how attractive Brian is, there's no way that he sees me as anything but an employee, so really there's no reason to say no.

"Let's do it, roomie," I say, giving him a weak smile before closing my eyes and leaning back against my seat, wondering what in the hell I did to end up in this situation.

By the time we make it back to Deer Valley Inn, I feel like I'm going to be sick off the nerves and anxiety bouncing around in my stomach.

"I'll just run in and grab your stuff. Bridget said she grabbed everything she saw before they closed it off, so let's hope it's enough to get you through. Plus, I need to grab some paperwork I left in my office. I'll be right back," he says, jumping out of the truck and making his way inside before I have a chance to respond.

I look around and try to focus on anything that might take my mind off the fact that I'll apparently be living with my incredibly sexy boss. I spend a few minutes fidgeting in my seat until I'm unable to sit still any longer. I know Lizzie is probably asleep since it's almost midnight in Paris, but I can't resist sending her a text anyway.

> Me: Buckle up cause I've got a story for you...

I start to sit my phone down, but it immediately pings with an incoming text.

> Lizzie: Spill now please!

> Me: Soooo apparently either I'm on Santa's shit list or I have the worst luck in the world.

> Me: My room at the inn flooded...

> Lizzie: Oh my God, are you okay?!

> Lizzie: What are you going to do?!

> Lizzie: Do they have any extra rooms?

> Me: No they don't. So apparently I'm moving in with my new boss...

Lizzie: SHUT UP

Lizzie: YOU'RE LYING

Lizzie: I DON'T BELIEVE YOU

Me: I swear. He went in to grab my stuff. We're waiting to see if anything opens up around town, but until then I don't have anywhere to go.

Lizzie: MILLIE!

Lizzie: This is a Christmas miracle!

Lizzie: Please tell me you're gonna ride him like he's Santa's sleigh!

Me: Lizzie, he's still my boss. And I can't. I'm sure he's not interested anyway.

Lizzie: Bull shit. I bet you anything that before Christmas Eve you two are obsessed with each other.

Me: Yeah, yeah. Love you big, sis.

Lizzie: Love you bigger. Send me all the updates.

I spend the next few minutes daydreaming about how it would feel to have Brian the way my sister's insinuating and feel my body heat at the thought.

God, I'm gonna lose it. I can't keep worrying about this, or I'll go crazy.

Deciding to focus on something other than my attraction to my incredibly hot boss, I tuck my phone away and reach to the floor for my bag. Pulling out my planner, I flip it open and start creating a to-do list for all the things I need to get done over the next week before the maze.

Arrange shuttles between the inn and the maze.
Make sure the kitchen has the supplies for the cookies.
Set up the decorations at the tree farm.
Reach out to volunteers.
Ignore the fact that my new roommate might be the sexiest man I've ever laid eyes on.

Easy enough, right?

CHAPTER 9

BRIAN

When we finally roll into my driveway, I'm exhausted and on edge.

Spending the entire day with Millie was pure torture. Not because she isn't good company—quite the opposite, actually. I don't remember the last time I enjoyed a road trip as much as I did today. Not only is she fucking gorgeous, but her ideas for the inn are genius and she's funny as hell. Spending hours inhaling her vanilla perfume and catching glimpses of her curves has literally eaten away at every bit of control that I possess, begging me to forget the fact that she's my employee. All afternoon I told myself I just had to make it to this evening, then I could drop her off and regroup. But instead, here she is sitting in my driveway because I opened my big mouth and couldn't let her leave town.

God, this is gonna be a disaster, but it's too late now to do anything about it.

"Home sweet home," I say, trying to lighten the tension that suddenly feels suffocating.

"Brian, I really appreciate this, but are you sure you don't mind? I can see about staying somewhere else. The last thing I want to do is make you uncomfortable after everything you've done for me," she says, looking sheepish.

"Yes, I'm sure, Millie. There aren't many options in Springside to begin with, and combined with the weather and the holidays, there isn't anywhere else for you to go. Plus, I have plenty of room," I tell her, jumping out of the car and reaching in the back to grab her bags.

We walk in silence to my front door, and after fidgeting with the lock, I open it and lead her inside. I forgot to leave any lights on when I left this morning, and it's so dark I can barely see anything. I move to find the light switch, but when I flip the first switch nothing happens.

Weird.

I notice the faint glow of the clock in the kitchen, so I know the power isn't out. Assuming the lightbulb must have blown since I can't remember the last time I changed it, I go to step further into the house reaching my hands out in front of me for the lamp I keep in the living room.

Instead of the lamp, I feel a soft brush of skin followed by Millie's sharp intake of breath. I tell myself to move my hand, but I feel frozen, finally feeling her skin grazing my hand. After thinking about her constantly for the last day, all I want in this moment is to pin her against the wall and taste her sweet mouth against mine.

We stand frozen in the darkness, like both of us are scared to break the spell we're under. I feel her lean slightly into my touch, and any bit of control I had snaps. Before I know what I'm doing I'm leaning against her, desperate to claim her lips. It's been years since I felt this level of need surging through me. Her breath quickens and my dick hardens in my pants, desperate to rub against her. I'm close enough that her hot breath grazes across my cheek. My lips brush against her mouth just as my phone rings, breaking us from our spell.

I hold back the curse that wants to break free before stepping away from Millie and checking my phone. The screen lights the room to show the name of one of the city councilmen that often calls to chat, but I have no desire to talk to him after what he just interrupted.

While I'm sending them to voicemail, Millie reaches for the lamp—thanks to the light from my phone screen—and flips the switch, causing light to filter through the dark space. We stare at each other in silence, neither of us willing to address what almost just happened between us.

Trying to break the uncomfortable quiet filling the room, I say, "So, uhh, let me give you a quick tour. Here's the living room and kitchen, the guest bedroom and bathroom are on the right. The laundry room is next to the back door, and my room is to the left, right across the hall from yours."

She looks at me, giving me another awkward smile before responding. "Oh great, thank you. I know I told you before, but I really appreciate you letting me crash here."

"Millie, you don't have to thank me. I'm sorry you can't stay at the inn right now. But I'm glad you're here. God knows I need someone to run these events. So really, you're doing me a favor," I tease.

Another blush covers her cheeks before she says, "Well I really am grateful, but I'm wiped. So let me grab my bag, and I'll be off to bed," she tells me, and it's impossible to deny the exhaustion creeping into her voice.

"Sure thing. Here, I've got it," I say, grabbing her bag from the floor where I dropped it before our encounter. "I'll walk you to your room."

We walk the short distance to the guest room, and I try to ignore the fact that she'll be sleeping this close to me for the foreseeable future. It would be so easy to suggest that she slip into my king-size bed instead, but I remind myself that I still have to behave, even if we aren't at the inn.

I'm so lost in thought, I don't realize she's leaning against the door when I go to sit her bag inside, and her body presses against mine for a few moments, before she pulls back.

"Oh, uh, sorry about that. Uhh, I'll drive us to the inn tomorrow morning. Just come out when you're ready. I usually leave around eight. Goodnight, Millie," I say in a rush, desperate to get away from her and get my thoughts under control.

"Goodnight, Brian," she says, before hastily retreating to her newly claimed bedroom and closing the door without a second glance.

I lean against the wall, fighting the urge to pull at my hair. Damn it, that was not how tonight was supposed to go. God, it's been a long time since I felt this rattled by a single almost kiss, but my pulse is still racing, and my hands are longing to pull her against me and kiss her mouth the way I want to.

I give into the moment and let myself imagine the taste of her lips and the feel of her soft curves under my hands. I think about all the times earlier today when I had to remind myself to be a professional and let out a low growl of frustration. The door looks back at me, daring me to knock and finish what we almost started in the dark a few minutes earlier. After fantasizing for another minute, I turn and walk toward my bedroom, throwing myself on the bed and rubbing my hand down my face.

Yeah, clearly the whole roommate idea was a genius plan. What else could go wrong?

CHAPTER 10

MILLIE

Oh my God! What the hell was that? Did he mean to almost kiss me? There's no way. It had to have been an accident. Right?

I've spent the entire night tossing and turning, trying to figure out what on earth just happened. I know I should be thankful his phone brought us out of whatever spell we were under, but God, I was desperate to feel his lips on mine.

I groan when I look over at the clock in the corner and see that it's almost six in the morning. When we pulled into the driveway last night, I'd been ready to collapse as soon as I walked through the door, but after the almost kiss, I haven't been able to stay still for more than a few minutes at the time. I might have dozed for thirty minutes at the most, and I know the restless energy in my body isn't going to let me rest any more.

God, today's gonna suck, I think with a grimace, before pulling myself out of the bed. *Oh well, might as well get up and try to be productive.*

Digging through my bag, I throw on a pair of leggings and a long-sleeve running top before hunting for my tennis shoes. After slipping them on, I toss my hair into a ponytail, grab my phone, and open my door to head out for a run.

When living in D.C., this had become a regular part of my routine when I needed to clear my head. It was probably the only thing I've done for myself over the last few years, and while I've never been particularly fast, I love the opportunity it gives me to organize my thoughts.

The house is dark and silent as I make my way outside, so I assume Brian is still asleep. Not wanting to wake him with a text, I scribble out a note on a piece of scratch paper.

Going for a run. Be back around seven. Call if you need me.

Grabbing a bottle of water from the fridge, I head outside and do some quick stretches before taking off. I don't really know where I'm going, but Brian's neighborhood seems safe, so I decide to just make a couple loops around the block to make sure I don't get lost.

The sun is starting to rise, and I smile at the array of colors in the cold morning as I finish my warm-up and start to push into my first sprint of the day. I'm just starting to gain speed when I hear an unfamiliar voice from one of the houses across the street. "My, my, you must be the new event planner, huh?"

Startled, I look to my left where I see an elderly lady I don't recognize sitting out on her porch with a cup of coffee. She gives me a smile and says, "Millie, right?"

My face must show my shock, because the old lady lets out a cackle and continues. "I guess no one's warned you how fast word travels around here. I'm Miss Ethel. Welcome to Spring-side, hun."

I stare at her for another minute trying to figure out the best way to handle the situation, before finally saying, "Uhh, yeah. How did you know my name?"

Ethel lets out another laugh before she says, "Oh, hun, word was out about you probably about the time you hit that deer and totaled your car. We don't get newcomers around here too often, but we're real glad you're here."

Wait, not only does this woman know my name but she also knows about the wreck?

I'm contemplating making a run for it despite the fact that I'm confident I could take her if I really needed to, but instead I ask, "Umm okay. Good to know, I guess… What are you doing out here so early, Miss Ethel?"

"Oh, dear, I love watching the neighborhood come alive in the morning. Plus, how else would I get all the gossip? Seeing who's sneaking where is a good way to make sure I don't miss anything," she says with a laugh.

My God. This woman wasn't kidding. I briefly recall Huey's warning about the "nosey sons of bitches" around town, and fight to laugh at the absurdity of this little town.

"Oh, I gotcha. Well, it's nice to meet you, Miss Ethel. I'm sure I'll see you around," I say, ready to return to my run.

"Oh yes, dear, I'm sure you will. Excited to see what you do with our Christmas events this year," she says with a smile. "I'm on the Gingerbread Gala committee, so we'll have to chat soon."

Great, can't wait for that. By then you'll probably know the name of the dog I had when I was in middle school and my high school GPA. With that, I nod and give her a polite wave before returning to my run.

I try to block out the world and organize my thoughts as I run but after a lap around the block, I can't help feeling like there are eyes on me. After taking in my surroundings, I realize that almost every house I pass suddenly has someone sitting on their front porch. Some are sipping coffee and pretending to be preoccupied with something on their phone, but most are openly staring at me as I pass.

I look ahead to see another older woman standing in her driveway a few feet ahead and waving her hands to flag me down. *God, what's a woman gotta do to run in peace around here?*

Without anywhere else to go, I slow to another stop and pause my playlist.

"You're the new high falutin' visitor from the city, huh?" she asks, looking me up and down.

"Uhh, yeeaaahhh, I guess so," I say, uncomfortable with the look of disdain on her face.

"Listen here, girl. Everyone here may be content to buy your story but I'm onto you… If you think you're gonna slip in and scope out our city for that supposed 'ex' husband of yours, you've got another thing coming. We don't need some big city real estate company trying to come in and take over our city," she says angrily, adding in some air quotes around the ex-husband comment as if she's trying to emphasize her point.

I stare at her stunned for a moment. Is this woman for real? She's clearly watched one too many Hallmark Christmas movie marathons.

"I'm sorry, I must have missed your name," I say as I try to come up with a response for the outlandish accusation she just threw at me.

"I'm Miss Sally. And just know, y'all will never get away with your little plan," she says, before throwing another dirty look my way and turning to make her way back inside.

Ahhh, yep. I'm with Brian. If this is her normal behavior, she totally deserves to have her house rolled.

Shaking my head, unable to believe that the previous conversation actually happened, I take off again, needing to burn some of my angry energy. As I get going, I see more people outside, pretending like they aren't looking at me. I try to tell myself that this is probably their usual morning routine, but when I pass a lady that looks like she's in her eighties trying to take a picture of me, I've hit my limit.

This place is actually insane… Where on earth did I break down?

Annoyed that even my runs aren't free from the chaos of this town, I decide to give it up for today even though the mile and a half I've covered isn't even a quarter of what I normally need to quiet my anxious thoughts.

I'm walking through the front door when I see Brian sitting at the kitchen bar looking over some emails and drinking a cup of coffee, reminding me of the initial reason I needed to move my body this morning. He's wearing pajama pants and a long sleeve T-shirt, and his hair is still tousled from sleep. On top of that, he's wearing a pair of glasses that make him look even sexier, which, before now, I wouldn't have thought was possible.

"Good morning," I say, my voice coming out angrier with frustration than intended.

"Good morning, Millie. Everything okay?" he asks, and I fight the urge to smile despite my annoyance at the sound of concern in his voice.

"Oh yeah, everything's wonderful except for the fact that everyone in this neighborhood has lost their mind. I tried to go on a run and it started with a lady who could be my grand-mother knowing all about me and it ended with all of your neighbors sitting outside on their porches watching me. One at the end was even trying to take my picture!" I exclaim incredu-lously before adding, "Oh, and I had the pleasure of meeting Miss Sally too. She's actually horrible!"

"Wait, what did Miss Sally do?" he questions, his concern already turning to anger.

"That woman has lost it. She accused me of basically breaking down here on purpose so that I could get the inside scoop for my ex-husband. I guess she thinks we're gonna turn main street into a shopping mall or some other Hallmark bullshit."

At that, Brian stands, and I can feel the fury rolling off him. "What the actual hell? Stay here, I'm going to talk to her right now."

I try to ignore the twist my heart gives at his protectiveness but completely fail. Through the entire time Allen and I were married, he never once defended me, even when his friends called me white trash and other derogatory names. They thought that because I'd attended public school and needed scholarships to attend college, I wasn't as good as they were. But here Brian is, only a few days after meeting me, ready to run down the street to defend me.

"No, no. You don't need to do that! Anyway, how did the other neighbor know so much about me?" I ask, trying to distract him from causing a scene he'll definitely regret once he calms down.

Brian lets out a groan. "Let me guess, Miss Ethel caught you first thing too, huh?"

"Oh my gosh, how'd you know?"

"She's pretty notorious in this neighborhood for sticking her nose where it doesn't belong. She probably sent out a STS alert as soon as she saw you step out the front door."

"What in the ever-loving hell is the STS?" I ask, feeling lost.

"Basically, it's an email thread that the old ladies use to share all the gossip," Brian explains with a grimace. "And considering the fact that I've made it a point to never have a woman over because this town is nosey as hell, they're probably losing their mind with theories about us."

"Great. So not only am I the new out-of-towner, I'm also about to be the new-in-town hussy," I whine. "It's over, I should just get out now, I guess. There's no coming back from this."

Brian looks at me seriously. "Millie, it's fine. I'll mention something about how you're staying here because of the water issue at the inn really loudly when I go to the post office this afternoon, if it would make you feel better. That's one of their favorite places to stand around and gossip. After that, there'll probably be at least ten little old ladies offering to take you in."

"Nope, I'm good on that front, thanks. I'm pretty certain Miss Ethel worked for the CIA or something in a past life, and she freaks me the heck out," I say with a laugh.

"I guess this didn't happen in D.C.?" he asks with a smirk.

"Uhh, that's the understatement of the decade. I lived in our penthouse in D.C. for ten years and I still couldn't tell you a single thing about anyone who lived in the building, but I've been here less than forty-eight hours, and everyone knows my entire life story. I'm sure they're all lovely people...except for Miss Sally, obviously, but anyway, I just wasn't expecting the Springside paparazzi on my morning run."

Brian laughs at my outburst and shakes his head. "Damn, yeah I guess when you look at it that way, this is a bit of an experience."

"Yeah, you could say so. Anyway, give me a few minutes to shower, and I'll be ready for work. I'll meet you back out here before eight."

"Sounds good. There's coffee in the pot. I'll be here when you're ready. See you then," he replies before turning back to his emails.

"So, I feel like I should warn you," Brian says with a wince as we pull into the parking lot of Deer Valley an hour later. "Miss Ethel, Miss Sally, and my nosey neighbors probably aren't the only ones in town who'll be wanting to know all about you. I'm hoping they'll all be on their best behavior, but as you saw this morning, the people in this town tend to have trouble minding their own business."

"You don't say," I mutter under my breath.

"Just know they don't have bad intentions, but they tend to get a bit over excited about newcomers. Just think, the last guy insulted Huey during his first day as the fire chief, so they hated him at first. You're off to a much better start than he was."

"What do you mean he insulted Huey? How rude!" I say, feeling suddenly protective of the older gentleman.

Brian lets out a laugh at my reaction as we get out of the car.

"It was all a big misunderstanding, and he and Huey are great friends now. Anyway, just promise me you won't go running for the hills if they all turn up today."

"Ugh, I promise. But just so you know, this town is not normal. At least I can grab some coffee before—" I say just before we enter the inn, where there are at least twenty people standing around the fire.

"Good morning, Mayor," one of them calls out. All the eyes turn to stare at us as we approach, and all the conversations they'd been having before our entrance come to an abrupt halt.

Are all these people seriously here because of me? Surely not, right?

"Good morning, Wayne," Brian responds. "What are y'all up to this morning?"

"Well, we thought we'd grab lunch at the restaurant," the man responds, and the crowd behind him nods.

"Yeah, we've heard great things about the Christmas specials y'all are trying out," one of the women adds.

"Hmm, y'all do realize it's not even nine in the morning, right?" Brian questions, raising his eyebrow.

"Oh, umm, yeah. We, uhhh, just wanted to make sure we didn't have to wait too long, you know? I've heard y'all are wrapped up with that snowstorm we had come through," another responds.

Brian lets out a chuckle before saying, "Oh right. So all of you decided to come to lunch for the first time ever, just by chance?"

Several in the group steal guilty glances at each other before just nodding back at him. *Well, I guess that answers that. This town is seriously on another level.*

"Awesome, well in that case, we'll leave y'all to your wait then. We've got a meeting to get to," Brian says, motioning for me to lead the way to his office.

Before I can move, one of the ladies pipes up, "You must be Millie! Welcome to Springside!"

I look to Brian, and after a moment, we both burst into laughter at the absurdity of the morning.

"Yeah, Christmas specials my ass," Brian says, shaking his head. "Y'all are really something else. Come on, Millie, we don't have to give in to their craziness," he says, reaching to pull me around them, and while I appreciate that he's giving me an out, the antics of this town are growing on me rapidly. Plus, it doesn't seem like it's gonna stop anytime soon, so I may as well learn to embrace it.

"No, no, it's fine," I tell him before turning back to the crowd in front of us. "Hey, everyone, I'm Millie. It's nice to meet y'all."

The next twenty minutes are a flurry of people introducing themselves and asking questions about everything from living in D.C., to my totaled car.

Damn, these people really did their research, I think to myself as one asks me if we had a good trip to Saddle Ridge yesterday.

After a few more minutes, Brian finally says, "All right, y'all got what you wanted. I expect a full report on how your lunch was when I see you at the Cattlemen's breakfast next week, Wayne. Hopefully, it's worth the wait."

"Sure thing," the older man says, tipping his hat at us as we walk to the office to get started for the day. Settling into the over-stuffed armchair in the corner and pulling out my notebook, I can't resist the urge to smile. Damn, despite the craziness of my arrival I have to admit, I think this town is gonna be a fun new adventure.

CHAPTER 11

BRIAN

"Y'all ready for tomorrow?" Huey asks through the phone speaker, while I fix myself a cup of coffee later the following week. It's the morning before the maze, and I'm confident Millie and I will both be running on copious amounts of caffeine today getting everything set up.

"Yeah, I think so. Millie's done a great job getting everything organized, so I think it'll be a fun event. You planning to come?" I question before taking a long sip of my drink.

"I'll be there with bells on," he says, and I laugh because I wouldn't be surprised if he meant it literally. "I meant to ask you yesterday, have you heard anything else about the insurance adjuster for the inn?"

"No. I've called, and John said they're still trying to get caught up from all the damages the snow caused last week. When Bridget talked to him, he said apparently we weren't the only people this happened to, and combined with all the vehicle accidents and the holidays, they'll be backed up for a couple weeks."

"Huh, well at least it was just the one room. I'm sure they'll get you sorted out. Anyway, I've gotta go check on the cows so I'll see you two tonight."

"See you then," I say, ending the call, and trying not to think about the woman who's consumed all of my thoughts recently.

Millie's been living in my house for eight days, and each day I'm convinced there's no way I can go another minute without her. We've settled into a routine, and it's driving me wild how badly I want her. We ride to work together, spend the day working on the upcoming events late into the night, ride back home, and go to bed just to do it all over again the next day.

Neither of us has brought up the almost kiss from last week, and I've tried telling myself that it's for the best. But every time her face lights up in excitement about an idea or I catch a whiff of her perfume, I can't control the desire that runs through me. Before the moment in the dark, I'd thought she was beautiful, but after the other night, she's consuming me.

As I wait for Millie to come out of her room after her run, I give myself my daily pep talk.

Get it together. She's not interested, and if you run her off because you're acting like a horny teenager, you'll never forgive yourself. You've never needed a woman before, and there's no reason to start now.

But when she walks out of my guest room in a festive red sweater and jeans that accentuate her curves, it feels like all my resolve goes right out of the window.

"Good morning," she says, giving me a small smile.

"Good morning. You ready for tomorrow? Your first official Springside Christmas event," I say, trying to distract myself from the way her red lipstick makes me want to claim her mouth.

"Yeah, I am. I can't believe it's already here. I keep worrying I'll forget something, but I've checked my to-do list at least a hundred times. Hopefully we're good to go," she replies.

"I'm sure it'll be perfect. The kids will love the activities you added in for them, and the decorations look incredible. I can't believe how much you've gotten done in the last week," I admit honestly. And while I'm trying to distract myself from how badly I'm craving her, I really have been blown away by how hard she's worked.

When I offered her the job, I didn't really know what to expect, but after seeing her in action this week, I've started to feel like she's probably vastly overqualified for the job at our little inn. Over the last week, she's ordered snow globe bouncy houses, created a mistletoe themed ornament station, and repurposed some old decorations from the storage room to make a huge photo wall, in addition to all the other tasks we discussed during our first meeting.

"Thank you," she says, taking the travel mug of coffee I'm holding out for her. "Now to just hang the last of the lights at Deer Valley and make sure everything's ready to go at the tree farm for tomorrow. I'm ready when you are."

"Sounds good," I say, grabbing my computer bag and throwing it over my shoulder. "Do you want to start at the inn or the maze?"

"Let's hit the inn first. I want to add some more of those pink ornaments and those stems I found online to the tree before we hang the lights," she says, and I nod making the drive to the inn.

"I'm grabbing our lattes and then I'll be ready to go over the final list with Bridget. Be right back," she says as soon as we step through the entrance, as we both wave hello to the usual group of locals that have taken to spending time in our lobby over the last week.

I just nod, hoping she doesn't notice my grimace. *These God forsaken cinnamon drinks are the bane of my existence*, I think to myself, as she bounces around the corner to the small café.

Each day is the same, and every time I've opened my mouth to tell her to stop, I catch a glimpse of the smile on her face as she hands me the disgusting concoction. Needless to say, I'm suffering through a few miserable sips each day until I can throw it away without her noticing.

After Millie bounds back into the office with our coffees, she and Bridget review the last few details for the day. Then she sets to work shoving an obscene amount of ornaments into the tree while I respond to emails signing off on the upcoming performance reviews for the city's horticulture department. Several hours pass while we work in silence, and I try to keep my gaze from wandering from my computer screen to where she's humming and decorating the lobby.

I've rechecked my to-do list and both my inn and the city emails respectively at least ten times. Not because I don't want to spend time with Millie, but because I know if I can't keep myself from watching her too closely, I'll never get anything done. Finally, after wasting another thirty minutes flipping between tabs on my computer screen, I stand and make my way over to her.

"You ready to head over to the maze?" I ask, once again shocked by how incredible she's managed to make everything look. This morning, the lobby looked festive enough, but this afternoon it looks like it's ready for a feature in *Southern Living*. The tree sparkles with the extra stems and ornaments she tucked into the branches, and she's added greenery and boxwood wreaths above the fireplace and at the front desk. "It looks incredible."

"Thanks," she says, and I chuckle at the glitter clinging to her face and clothes. "I swear, I'll be finding glitter in my clothes for the next three months."

I laugh as we make our exit and ride in comfortable silence over to the Coopers' Christmas Tree Farm, which Millie has also transformed into a complete winter wonderland with fake snow.

Yesterday afternoon, she'd coordinated a group of volunteers to set up most of the larger decorations while I attended the monthly city council meeting. I hated to leave her with it for a few hours, but considering the fact that I've neglected almost all of my mayoral duties since she arrived in town, I begrudgingly listened while the councilmen argued about the color for the new benches we agreed to place in city park.

But thanks to Millie's hard work and the help of her volunteers, all that's left today is to string the lights through the trees at the entrance and exit, since the Coopers offered to take care of the inside. They had a way of lighting the way of different paths with certain colors to make sure no one got lost, and I was thankful we didn't have to worry about that headache.

By the time we get everything unloaded, the sun is starting to set, and the air is getting cooler. Millie checks her phone and lets out a groan.

"What's wrong?" I ask while lining up the extension cords we'll need to cover the line of trees on either side.

"I just got texts from five different volunteers saying stuff came up, and they can't make it tonight. We're never gonna get this done," she proclaims, looking at the forty something trees stretching in front of us that we're supposed to be covering in lights.

"Did they say what came up?" I ask, knowing it's pretty out of character for the group to cancel this short of notice.

"Uhh, kind of a mix of reasons. Apparently there's a stomach bug going around and Caroline said she needed to help Theo get Petunia back in the pen after she made an escape... Who the hell is Petunia? Their dog?" she responds, and I can't help but burst into laughter.

"Theo moved into town earlier this year to replace Huey as the fire chief, and he bought a bunch of farmland to get some animals. Huey set him up with one of the local farmers who was looking to sell some of their livestock, but Mr. Willy convinced him to take his temperamental donkey named Petunia. Let's just say she really lives up to the whole ass title," I explain, and Millie dissolves into a fit of giggles.

"I swear, this town..." she says as she tries to regain her composure.

"Tell me about it. Anyway, let me see if I can call in some reinforcements," I say, picking up my phone and trying a few of our usual volunteers, only to get their voicemails. I send out a few texts too, but no one responds right away. "All righty then, that was a failure, but we can do this. Grab a few strands and we'll get started. Maybe a couple more will show up later."

Millie nods and walks over to the truck to grab several boxes of the lights we bought last week in Saddle Ridge while I unload the ladder.

"I was thinking we could start here and work our way down. The Coopers showed me how they usually run the extension cords too, so I'll go plug the first one in," Millie suggests, leaving me to start unwrapping the first box of lights.

Once she returns, we grab the ladder, and she pauses for a moment, looking for the best system of draping the trees. "I think if you'll unroll them, I can stand up here and place them. With your height, you can hand me the ones from the back and hopefully we can be done in a couple hours."

"Sounds good," I respond, realizing that setting up over one hundred boxes of lights isn't the biggest challenge of the evening. We'll be brushing against each other over and over in the dark while I try to keep my hands to myself. *Awesome.*

AFTER TWO HOURS, WE'VE MANAGED TO MAKE IT THROUGH HALF THE trees, but we're both freezing, hungry, and ready to go home.

"I've gotta say, I thought winters in Alabama were supposed to be warm," she says, and I notice her hands have started shaking. "I swear it's dropped at least twenty degrees since we started."

"Yeah, I think you're right. We can't stay out in this cold all night. We're not exactly dressed for the elements," I remark, gesturing to our thin sweaters and jeans. "Let's finish the back of this one, and then I'll get someone out here to help me tomorrow while you're setting up at the inn."

"Are you sure?" she asks, the crinkle of concern in her brow making me want to reach out and smooth it.

Instead, I nod and say, "Of course. Now let's get this knocked out. I'm starving," while grabbing another strand of lights and holding it out for her.

She leans to grab it, but as soon as I hand it off, it slips through her fingers, and she reaches for it on instinct. The moment seems like it happens in slow motion as I watch the ladder topple, and Millie falls toward the cold ground. Before I can give myself time to think, I'm grabbing for any part of her that I can reach and pulling her toward me. All I can think about is keeping her from hitting the ground.

"I've got ya," I say as I try to catch her, but in reality, I just manage to break her fall. We tumble down, and she lands on my chest as I wrap my arms around her. Thankfully she was only a few feet off the ground, but the fall is enough to knock the wind out of both of us. We lie there with her on top of me for a moment, both of us breathing hard.

"Oh my gosh, thank you," she says, as a gust of wind blows a piece of hair into her face.

I reach up and push it back, holding my hand behind her head. It would be so easy to press her mouth to mine in this scenario. Her lips are still red from the lipstick she applied this morning, and I can already imagine how good they would feel all over me. Her legs are straddling me, and I try to ignore the fact that her center is inches away from my hardening cock.

To my surprise, she shifts toward me, and I wonder if she's trying to pull herself off me. Instead, she leans in a bit, neither of us taking our eyes off each other until she's hovering right in over me. My breath catches as she pauses, and I realize she's waiting for me to stop her.

Ha ha, yeah, right. All I can think about is exploring her body, after all the times over the last week I've thought about her. My arm around her back pulls her closer, and I thread my fingers through her hair leading her lips to mine.

She lets out a breathy moan as she shifts against me realizing how hard I am for her, and suddenly we're pouncing at each other. Our mouths clash, and I groan at the relief of finally feeling her lips against mine. She tastes like the sugar cookies we snacked on earlier at the inn, and her kiss is needy as if she's wanted this as badly as I have.

Unable to help myself, I wrap my hand around the front of her throat.

As soon as she feels my hand press against her neck, she lets out a moan. Damn, I didn't expect that reaction but fuck if it doesn't drive me wild.

Damn, this girl couldn't be more perfect.

I feel her grind against me as my hand slips under her sweater and I trace my hands up her back, kissing her hard. After a moment, I pull back, starting to kiss down her neck, desperate to feel every part of her.

"Brian? Millie? Y'all still out here?" I hear just as I register the sound of footsteps coming our way.

Immediately, Millie and I break apart and scramble up, just as Will Johnson steps around the tree we were hidden behind.

"Shit man, are y'all okay?" he asks, gesturing to the ladder that's still on the ground. "I saw your text for help and came by to see if you still needed anything."

Will's the football coach for Springside, and while we've always gotten along, I'd really like to punch him for interrupting the moment Millie and I were just having. I glance over at her but can't seem to catch her eye before turning back to Will. "Uhh, oh yeah. We're good. Millie here just tried to take a tumble, but I caught her. Thank you for coming over. We were just about to call it a night, but if you want to help out, I bet we could get another couple of these trees done."

"Oh, well, glad you caught her. Hey, Millie, I'm Will. I've heard a lot about you over the last week, but it's nice to meet you in person," he says, sticking out his hand for her to shake.

"Hi, it's nice to meet you as well," she says, giving him a smile.

"Sorry, I would have been here sooner, but I didn't hear my phone until just a few minutes ago. I'm down to help y'all get a few of these knocked out. Put me to work," Will says, rubbing his hands together.

"Why don't you take over the ladder duty," Millie says, bending down and opening another strand of lights. "I've had enough heights for today."

"No problem," he says, bending down and righting the fallen ladder.

"Thanks, um, I hate to ask but you don't happen to have any extra jackets in your truck, do you? I'm freezing, and Brian and I both forgot ours," Millie asks.

"Actually, I do. I parked right beside Brian. I think there are some blankets in there too. Go grab whatever you want," he offers, reaching in his pocket and tossing the keys in her direction.

As she walks away, Will and I work quietly for a moment before he smirks in my direction. "So, you wanna talk about it?"

"Talk about what?" I ask, waiting to see what he means.

"Man, come on. You've got dirt and shit all over your back, and there's bright red lipstick on your face. What the hell did I just walk up on?" Will asks, shooting me a knowing smirk.

Shit. Busted.

"Uhh, yeah." I groan, rubbing my hand over my face. "I don't know. That woman is driving me crazy. I'm trying to stay away because of the whole workplace thing, but God, I want her so bad."

Will nods looking like he's thinking about something else, before he just nods. "I get it man, I swear I do. But I don't think you're gonna know for sure until you go for it. Isn't y'all's whole arrangement only guaranteed through Christmas anyway?"

Shit, I can't believe I haven't thought about that. Millie settled so easily into my life, and we've been so consumed with all things Christmas, that I haven't given it much thought that she might be planning to leave before the Christmas lights even come down.

He must read my expression, because Will just nods. "That's what I thought. I mean obviously don't pressure her if she's not into it, but it looks to me like you don't have anything to lose. Judging by the look on your face, you're gonna regret it if she drives away in two weeks, and you can't say you did everything to keep her."

Realizing he's right, I nod and open my mouth to say something else just as Millie returns.

"All right, y'all ready to get back to work?" she asks, and I tell myself to ignore the pang of jealousy I feel at seeing her wrapped in Will's oversized jacket.

We work for another hour while Millie and Will chat about her time in Springside. Finally, after we wrap the tenth tree, he says that he needs to head out. We've made great progress, and I feel confident I can finish the rest.

"Thanks for your help, Will. It was so nice meeting you. And thanks for letting me borrow this," Millie says, shrugging the jacket off and handing it back to him before looking toward me. "I'm gonna go unplug those cords since we're done for the night. I'll meet you back at the truck."

And with that she's gone, leaving Will and I standing in the trees, looking down at the big container filled with boxes of lights. "I'll help you get everything loaded up though," he says, leaning down and picking up the ladder while I grab the other supplies.

"Thanks, man. I appreciate it," I say, trying my best to sound sincere.

We make quick work of getting everything put away, and I wave at Will as he drives away, cranking the truck so it'll be warm.

While I wait on Millie to return, I shift anxiously. That was the most amazing kiss I've ever had in my life. I thought that if I tasted her, maybe the desire I was feeling would go away, but instead, I think it just made it worse. Will's words echo in my brain about not letting Millie go, and I decide he's right. I don't want to look back and wish that I'd gone after what I wanted if she decides to leave after the gala.

Now I'm just left to hope she feels the same way.

CHAPTER 12

MILLIE

When I hear the alarm go off the following morning, I groan in protest. *God, I swear I just closed my eyes.*

Once again, I'd spent the night tossing and turning, replaying the kiss with Brian. Last night was by far the hottest experience I've had in my life, which really tells me how pathetic my sex life with Allen was for the entirety of our marriage. The way Brian controlled the kiss made me desperate for him, but the enjoyment in the moment had been overshadowed by embarrassment.

God, not only did my clumsy ass fall on top of him, but I basically attacked him. I know I haven't had a job in a couple years, but I'm pretty sure most people don't make it a habit of dry humping their boss.

Groaning in embarrassment, I throw the covers off and start to get ready for the day. Having already decided to skip my run this morning knowing that it would be a long day, I grab my favorite pair of jeans and one of my new sweaters from Saddle Ridge and throw them on before spending some extra time on my makeup.

I tell myself the extra time I spend getting ready is because of the event tonight, but a large part of me knows that's only a small part of the truth. There's no way Brian doesn't regret kissing me.

My mind flashes to all the times I tried to initiate something physical with Allen throughout the last few years of our marriage. Every sneer, every eye roll, and every "maybe later, babe" is permanently ingrained in my thoughts, and I think about his comments he made about me during the divorce. That maybe if I was sexier or if I'd tried harder to keep him happy over the years, he wouldn't have had to screw his way through his staff.

I try to shake myself out of my mental pity party. Over the last week in Springside, it occurs to me that I've barely given Allen a single thought. There's no doubt this fresh start was exactly what I needed, but I'm not ready for Brian to give me the same look of rejection my ex-husband had perfected. He's been a perfect gentleman over the last few days, so I'm sure he'd be nicer about it than Allen always was, but the result will be the same.

Feeling frustrated, I hear my phone ping and grab it to see Lizzie just sent me a text.

> Lizzie: Hey sis, just checking on you? Are you ready to put that sexy boss of yours on the top of your Christmas list?

> Me: Hey, Lizzie. I'm okay…

> Lizzie: *eye roll emoji*

> Lizzie: I'm gonna need more than that.

> Lizzie: Have you and Mr. Mayor had any other run-ins?

I blow out a breath, trying to decide how to respond. I'd told her about the almost kiss last week over the phone two days ago, and she'd freaked out. I'm pretty sure my ears were still ringing from the way she squealed into the phone. She was convinced I'd be having kinky rebound sex by now and had become relentless about encouraging me to pursue him.

Gosh she's gonna lose her shit when I tell her what happened last night. Sighing, I decide to get it over with.

Me: Funny you should ask...

Me: There might have been a bit of an incident last night...

Lizzie: Mills, I swear to God if you don't spit it out I'm getting on a plane to kick your ass.

Me: Basically, I attacked him with my mouth. Afterward, he was a perfect gentleman and acted like it didn't happen. Soooo now I'm debating if I actually have to leave my room and face him today.

Lizzie: WHAT?!

Lizzie: You should really give a girl some warning... I just screamed so loud, the whole office heard.

Lizzie: But that's not important.

Lizzie: TELL ME EVERYTHING!!

Me: Ugh it's so embarrassing... All my volunteers had to cancel, so we were putting up the lights for the Mistletoe Maze tonight. I fell off the ladder and he tried to catch me. But we were both on the ground and he touched my hair, and I swear my brain left my body.

Me: Literally the best kiss of my life. God, it was so hot.

Me: But one of the locals interrupted us, and neither of us mentioned it after we got home.

Me: Oh my God, what if he fires me.

Me: Pretty sure Deer Valley doesn't have a head of HR, but I probably violated about a hundred boss/employee rules last night.

Lizzie: I KNEW IT!

Lizzie: Just calm down, it's gonna be fine.

Lizzie: He's not going to fire you.

Lizzie: So, are we talking about a kiss or a KISS?

Me: Ummmmmm…

Me: Sis, I literally dry humped my boss. On the ground. In a field.

Me: He also wrapped his hands around my throat, and I thought I was going to orgasm just from that.

Me: I thought that only happened in those romance novels we love, but nope. Can confirm it was incredibly hot.

Me: I'll let you do with that information what you will.

Lizzie: Hellllll yes.

Lizzie: Guess you're going on the naughty list this year ;)

Me: Lizzie!

Me: This is serious. What should I do?!

Lizzie: You mean other than bang his brains out?

Lizzie: Pretty sure that's the only right answer
here...

Lizzie: Shit, something just came up I have to
handle at work, but go get your man! I'll check
in with you tomorrow. Love you big.

Me: Yeah, yeah. Okay, love you bigger sis.

Throwing my phone back down, I fluff my hair in the reflection of my mirror and apply some lipstick. Lizzie might have been trying to make me feel better, but I can't help preparing myself for an uncomfortable encounter this morning.

After killing as much time as I can without making us late, I finally throw on a pair of boots and grab everything I need for the day before stepping out into the living room. Brian's on the phone, but he looks up at my entrance and gives me a smile, gesturing to a to-go cup full of coffee.

"Ready?" he mouths to me, still listening to whoever's on the other end of the line.

Nodding, we make our way out of the house and head to the inn. I wait for Brian to get off the phone and fire me or tell me what we did last night was wrong, but instead he spends the entire ride stuck on the phone. Oh well, I guess that means I'm still employed for the time being.

As soon as we arrive at the inn, I distract myself with preparing for the event, and the rest of the day is a blur of decorating and other last-minute tasks. Before I know it, it's close to seven and the lobby of Deer Valley is bustling with people. I catch Brian's eye just as I'm approached by a group of women led by Miss Ethel, and he gives me an encouraging smile.

"Millie, you were holding out on me," she teases, gesturing to the eight-foot Christmas tree I spent the last two days decorating. "Everything looks beautiful. I've never seen Deer Valley so festive. Now I need you to come decorate my house."

Several of the other ladies nod and murmur their agreement,

and I smile before responding, "Oh, y'all are too kind. Thank you, ladies."

"How are you enjoying your time in Springside dear?" one of them I haven't met yet asks.

"Oh, it's been wonderful. This town is really special," I answer truthfully.

"Yeah, you're right about that. So, Miss Millie, what do you think about our mayor?" another asks, and the whole group leans in, waiting to hear what I'll say.

"Umm, oh, uhh Mayor Jones has been very nice. I'm very grateful he gave me a chance when I broke down here. He's been very hospitable," I say, hoping that will assuage her curiosity.

"Hmmmm, I'll say. Aren't y'all living together?" someone else asks, and I feel my cheeks flame.

"I guess you could say so. My room at the inn had some damage, so he's letting me stay in his guest room."

"Well, isn't that kind of him? You know, he's one of Springside's most eligible bachelors... And you're recently divorced, aren't you?"

"Yeah, that's right."

"Oh, I see a royal wedding sometime in our future," one of the ladies says, while another offers, "Honey, you've gotta meet my grandson."

The group of ladies all start talking at once, and I'm pretty sure my face is frozen in a state of shock.

"All right, ladies, that's enough," Ethel says, shaking her head at her friends after realizing my surprise. "Damn old biddies, has no one ever told you to mind your own business?"

I fight the urge to laugh before Brian catches my attention and gestures to me.

"Well, it was lovely to chat with y'all, but I've gotta get back to work. Y'all enjoy the event," I tell the group of women in front of me, before slipping back over to where Brian is standing against the wall.

"Millie, everything looks incredible. This is the best turn out we've ever had, and it looks like everyone's really having a blast," he says, and I try not to pay too much attention to the way the compliment makes me feel giddy.

"Thanks, but I couldn't have done it without you," I tell him truthfully.

"Yeah, I guess we make a pretty good team. So, you ready for us to go ahead with the tree lighting? If so, I'll make the announcement for people to head outside," he asks.

"Sure, everything's ready to go. I'll make sure the speaker we set up is playing," I reply, zipping my jacket and preparing to step outside into the chilly evening.

"Oh, and Millie, you owe me a sleigh ride. Come find me when it's time to head over to the tree farm," he says.

"Yes, sir," I reply on instinct, and I don't miss the way his eyes flash at my statement as I rush outside. God, what the hell is wrong with me, and why can't I stop picturing using that phrase in a situation that's definitely not appropriate for work.

It takes what feels like forever to get everyone outside to light the tree. Eventually, Brian welcomes them and gives the countdown to light the community Christmas tree. The town cheers as the dark night fills with the glow of the multi-colored lights on the thirty-foot tree we brought in and settled into the ground this morning. I have to admit, the sight is beautiful, and while I've only been in Springside a few weeks, I can't help but feel like I'm home.

After a few minutes, the crowd starts to disperse. Some head inside for their dinner reservations, and others grab for the wine and cookies we're serving from a repurposed lemonade booth I found in the storage closet. The sleighs and trolleys pull up to take the first group of guests over to the maze, and I take a moment to appreciate how well everything seems to be going.

"There she is." I hear from behind me and turn to see Huey making his way over to where I'm standing with Brian at his side. "Millie, this is incredible. I felt like this job would be a good fit for ya, but I've never seen anything like this," he says before pulling me in for a hug.

"Oh, thank you, Huey, but I couldn't have done it without Brian's help," I say, gesturing to my boss.

"Yeah, yeah, well, listen, I've been slammed thanks to some trees that fell on my fence, but the two of you need to come over for supper next week," he insists.

"That sounds great. I need to see those cows again too," I say, and Huey laughs.

"I'm sure those heifers would love to see you again too. Just text me what night works best, okay? Anyway, there's some hot chocolate that's calling my name. I'll see y'all later," he calls out before disappearing into the slew of people in front of us.

Both of us shake our heads before Brian says, "You ready to go? Bridget is staying back to make sure everything runs smoothly here, but I figured you'd want to be there when the first group arrives."

"Yeah, that sounds good," I reply, letting him lead me to one of the smallest horse-drawn sleighs that's parked off to the side. There are two seats left, so we settle in and make small talk with the people beside us until one of the volunteers' waves from the driver's seat, signaling that we are about to start moving.

"Ugh, I'm seriously gonna need to upgrade my wardrobe," I joke as I shiver in the cold night air. "Alabama really should not be allowed to be this cold."

Brian laughs before reaching around and shrugging off his thick Carhartt jacket. "Here, my jacket's warmer. Why don't you throw it on?"

"But then you'll be the one shivering," I say hesitantly, even though I'm already reaching for the thick garment.

"Nah, I'm good," he states, holding it open for me to put my arms in. I pull it on and try not to react to being surrounded by his masculine scent. He always smells like cedar, and I fight the urge to bury my nose into the fabric.

We ride for a moment before I catch a glimpse at the lights ahead. Apparently, it's a Springside tradition for everyone to wait to show off their Christmas decor until the night of the Mistletoe Maze, so I'm completely taken aback when I see what seems to be an endless sea of lights. It's about two miles between the inn and the tree farm, and it looks like every inch of the route is covered with different colors and shapes of lights.

"God, it's beautiful," I breathe out, leaning against Brian to see around him.

"Yeah, it's a pretty special sight," he responds while I stare in awe at the shimmering display of colors.

"So, Millie, you've been in Springside for a few weeks now. What do you think about our little town?" he asks.

"I have to admit, it's really growing on me. Everyone, except maybe Miss Sally, has been really nice and I love planning these events. I know it sounds kind of cliché, but I really feel like I'm learning a lot about myself. I've been so scared for years to do anything just for me, but I'm seeing that I can support myself and go after the things I want. Basically, it's just what I didn't know I needed. I can't thank you enough for being so supportive and giving me a chance."

"Millie, you and I both know you're so overqualified for this job. You've been incredible," he says, and I don't miss the way my stomach flips at his words.

"Well…thanks," I say, feeling my cheeks redden with both the cold and the compliment. "Anyway, enough about me… Okay I've gotta know. You're a former football star, inn owner, and small-town mayor, right? Am I missing anything?" I tease.

"Nope, I think that about covers it," he responds, laughing at my outburst.

"Okay, I've just gotta ask, with all of that, how in the world are you still single?" I ask, only half joking.

He chuckles and I'm sure it's a question he gets often. He looks around to make sure the other locals aren't paying us any attention before explaining. "Well, to be really honest, my dad got sick right when I graduated from college, so I moved back home to help my mom take care of the inn. He spent three years going through treatments, and I can't say that dating was super high on my to-do list. Then a few years later, she got diagnosed with stage four brain cancer. It's weird how fast my priorities changed after that. Add in the responsibilities that come with running this town and trying to keep everything going, and I guess I just forgot to do something for myself."

God, do I understand that, I think, feeling a pang in my chest and immediately flashing back to how I felt losing my mom. She was the only family Lizzie and I had, and after we lost her, it seemed like everything that had been such major parts of our lives were insignificant. Decorating our tiny apartment for Christmas was always her favorite time of year, and I imagine for a moment about how much she would love this town. *It's been over ten years, but it never gets easier,* I think feeling a pang of sadness that she's not here to see it.

"Plus, in a town this small, options can be pretty limited. Everyone here's great, but there definitely haven't been any sparks with anyone here. At least, not until..." he starts, interrupting my pity party, just as we come to a stop at the tree farm.

But he doesn't finish because the driver of the sleigh turns to us with a big smile and says, "All right, everyone, enjoy the Midnight Mistletoe Maze."

Brian stands and helps me off the trolley. Immediately, we're back to work, running back and forth and chatting with the guests. But between snapping some pictures for the Instagram page I'm planning to ask to start for the inn and counting the profits from the mistletoe ornaments, I can't help but wonder how exactly he planned to finish that previous sentence.

CHAPTER 13

BRIAN

"Oh my goodness, Mayor, this is the most magnificent Mistletoe Maze we've ever had," Miss Agnes says as I help her to the trolley. "I don't know where you found that big city event planner, but you better do what you can to keep her. Just imagine what she could do for our Spring Flower Festival."

"Oh, yes, ma'am, I'll see what I can do," I say as I lead the elderly lady over to where a few of her friends are waiting to join the last shuttle back to Deer Valley.

"We'll put your walker back here, and the DD's will be waiting to take you home back at the inn. You ladies be safe and try to stay out of trouble," I tease, before making my way over to where Millie is standing back watching the last of the visitors pull out of the parking lot.

We've spent the last four hours mingling and making sure everyone had what they needed as they went through the maze and watching as everyone enjoyed the event. Millie's suggestions to add some other activities for the kids was a major hit, and the mistletoe keepsake ornaments turned out to be a great way to bring in some extra revenue. It's been a fun night, but I'm desperate for Millie and I to spend some time alone and finally have a chance to talk about that kiss.

"Well, I guess congratulations are in order, Miss Pouncey," I declare, leaning down to pull out the bottle of wine and glasses I'd snagged from the inn out of my bag. "You survived your first Springside Christmas event, and I must say I think it was a raging success."

"Thanks, Brian" she says, taking the now full glass and clinking it against mine. We both take a sip, and I gesture toward the maze.

"Come on, Mills, everyone's had a chance to go through. The last trolley just left, and the only people left here are the volunteers. Plus, the DD's will make sure everyone gets home. You're officially off duty for the night. Let's see if we can do it," I say, reaching out to pull her along with me.

I know I should keep my hands to myself until after we're able to sort out what happened last night, but I can't fight the urge to touch her any longer. We rode home in silence last night, neither of us sure how to break through the awkward tension of almost being caught kissing like teenagers, and while I'd hoped to talk to her this morning, I spent over two hours on the phone with one of the companies we'd hired to do some repairs at City Hall.

"Right or left?" I ask her as we come to the first split looking at the different colored trails that lead into different parts of the maze.

"Hmm, left. I can't believe as much time as we've spent out here this week that we haven't been through it yet," she says with a laugh.

"Left it is," I say, trying not to focus too much on the way the Christmas lights make her eyes shine.

We walk for another minute in silence, following the blue row of lights, showing us the path.

"So, Millie about last night—" I start, but stop when all of a sudden all of the lights around us go out.

Millie and I both freeze, caught off guard by the darkness around us. "I guess the volunteers thought everyone was out," Millie says quietly before taking out her phone. "I'll just call and ask them to turn them back on."

She hits a few buttons on her phone and holds it up to her ear, waiting for whoever she called to pick up. After hearing it go to voicemail, she tries a different number but doesn't have any luck with it either.

"Great. Those are the only two numbers I have saved, and my phone's about to die," she groans. "Do you have yours?"

"Umm, no. I left it in the truck to charge after we used it to play music," I say. "But the moon's pretty bright, and we can't be far from the exit. It'll be fine."

"You're right," she says with a pause. "So, um, you were saying…"

"Yeah, I just figured we should probably talk about last night," I say, as we continue walking, trying to gauge her reaction.

"Uhh, yeah, I'm sorry, Brian. I know I shouldn't—" she starts, and I have to fight the urge to reach out my hand and pull her to me. "I just, I know it was really inappropriate, and I…"

"I don't regret it Millie," I admit. "I'm sorry if I made you uncomfortable, but…"

"What? Made me uncomfortable? I'm the one who basically attacked you," she says dramatically, and I can't contain the laugh that escapes me.

"Millie, stop. Is that really what you think? God, we're a mess," I remark, pausing at the impact of what her words mean.

Wait, does this mean we both really want this? My cock hardens at the prospect of her wanting to pursue something, but I refuse to give in to my desire until it's crystal clear. I blink, trying to regain my composure, just as she stumbles against me in the dark. I reach out and steady her, trying to keep my distance but unable to keep my hands to myself any longer.

"Brian, what do you mean?" she asks, and I don't miss the way her voice sounds breathier than before.

"It means, Millie Pouncey, that I'm so desperate to have you that I don't know what to do with myself. But I know you're still processing all the change that's happened over the last few weeks, and I refuse to take advantage of the situation. I've made myself a promise that I'm not going to push you further until you tell me exactly what you want. But when you do, you better be ready, because my self-control can only go so far. Do you understand?" I growl, reaching through the darkness to finally pull her body into mine.

She gasps when she feels how hard I am for her, whispering, "W-w-what?"

"Yes, Miss Pouncey," I mutter, grazing my lips across hers. "If you decide you want something to happen between us, you're going to have to use your words. You're in control for now, got it? But if you say the word and I get my hands on you, I'm not stopping till you're sure you're mine."

"Oh, God," she groans before grabbing me by the front of my shirt and kissing me hard. Her arms skate around my neck, and she wraps one of her legs around my back, pulling me closer to rub against her.

My hands slide under her sweater, and I feel the smooth skin of her lower back, but it's not enough. I meant what I said, she's gonna have to instigate and ask for anything between us to happen. There's no way I can tell her no after the tension that's been building over the last few days.

I'm sliding my hands up, inches from finally feeling her full breasts against my hands, when the lights finally cut back on. We jump apart, and I fight the growl that wants to work its way through at being interrupted again.

"Um, that was…" she starts, looking dazed and running her fingers over the lips where my mouth was.

"Yeah, sure was," I agree. All I want is to pull her back to me and kiss her mouth, but as we stand beneath the lights, the moment seems lost. I debate reaching for her hand, but after having her body pressed against me, it doesn't seem like enough.

"Guess they got the lights back on," I say gloomily, folding my arms across my chest.

"Yeah, you ready to get going? It's already after midnight," she asks, starting to make her way toward the exit. I'm not sure if I'm imagining it, but I'm almost certain I hear the same disappointment in her voice that I'm feeling right now.

"Yep, I'm wiped," I say as we take a right at the next turn.

We walk for a moment, and we're almost to the end of the maze before she pauses and says, "Brian?"

I look over at her, and my heart skips a beat at the look in her eyes. She gestures to the canopy of mistletoe that's hanging over the exit. "Kiss me again, please."

God, I thought she'd never ask.

I lean down and plant a slow kiss on her mouth this time, knowing that my control will snap if I kiss her again like I did back there in the dark. This kiss is still needy, but instead of the rushed desperation I've felt the last two times I kissed her, this one is unhurried. It feels like taking our time to make sure that we don't break the spell we're under.

After a few minutes of tasting her, we pull back, both out of breath and dazed. "Come on, Mills, let's go home," I say, feeling a content smile spread across my face at the words.

CHAPTER 14

MILLIE

The sun coming through my window eventually pulls me from my slumber the following morning, and I roll over, savoring the feeling of waking up without an alarm. Last night on the way home, Brian insisted I take the day off and I accepted, eager for the opportunity to sleep in after all the early mornings and late nights we've had this week.

Rolling over, I grab my phone and see that I managed to sleep until almost nine. Noticing I have a few missed texts, I smile when I see Brian's already sent me something this morning.

Brian: Good morning. I'm running over to Saddle Ridge to meet with the contractor that's about to start working on the repairs for City Hall, but I'll be back this afternoon.

Brian: Also, I stopped by Deer Valley to grab some paperwork I left in the office on the way out of town and grabbed you a coffee. It's in the microwave when you get up. Enjoy your day off, and you better not let me catch you working. Relax today… that's an order.

My stomach dips at the tone of his text. It's incredible how fast he can go from being a perfect gentleman to a man who has me willing to drop my panties at the drop of a hat.

When he told me last night that he wasn't going to make a move until I asked him to, I'd been ready to drop to my knees and do whatever I needed to feel his hands all over me. But of course, we got interrupted again, and the last kiss we shared had been sweet and gentle compared to the last two, like he was determined to savor it. Then, on the way home, he was back to his usual polite demeanor, asking me about my favorite music and books before walking me to my room and telling me to spend the day in bed or doing whatever else I wanted. And now, he's sending me bossy texts and bringing me my favorite coffee...

Dear Lord, bless and strengthen any self-control left within me because I'm pretty sure it's so far gone, I think it might be halfway to Texas by now.

Me: Oh, that was sweet. You didn't have to do that.

Brian: I know I didn't have to, Millie. I wanted to.

Brian: Also, Huey called this morning. He wants to know if we're up for dinner tonight. I told him that would probably be fine, but I needed to check with you first. Does that work for you?

Me: Sure, that's fine. And thank you, Brian.

Brian: You're welcome Mills. Now, enjoy your day. I'll be home around four.

Me: Yes sir.

Clicking out of his messages, I see that I also have a few texts from my sister. Oh, God... Lizzie is going to go ballistic when I tell her what happened last night. Groaning, I tap her name, deciding I may as well get it over with. Plus, I wouldn't mind having her opinion on the situation because I'm pretty sure I'll drive myself crazy if I sit here reliving it all day by myself.

> Lizzie: Okay, sorry sis. I literally JUST got finished taking care of that fashion emergency. I need sleep and that IV of coffee Lorelei Gilmore was always talking about...

> Lizzie: BUT enough about me. I need updates on my favorite small town mayor.

> Lizzie: Please tell me something else happened...

Well, here we go.

> Me: Good morning! Dang, that sounds serious.

> Me: What happened at work?

> Lizzie: Oh, just something with one of our fabric manufacturers. I've spent the last twelve hours on the phone with the company in Switzerland trying to get it sorted.

> Lizzie: Stop trying to distract me though.

> Lizzie: What's happening between you and Mr. Mayor?

> Lizzie: Please tell me it's something dirty...

> Me: Ummmm...

I've barely sent the text before my phone lights up with an incoming call. Before I press it to my ear, I can already hear Lizzie's screech through the speaker.

"I knew it. You better start talking, or I swear to God..." she says, causing me to laugh.

"Well, hello to you too, sis," I say sarcastically.

"This is no time for small talk, Millie," she screams. "What the hell happened? I need details. I'm literally dying here."

"Okay, okay. My word, I'd totally hate for you to be dramatic," I tease. "But it's really not a big deal."

"Hmm, I think I'll be the judge of that. Now, spill!"

"Fine!" I say, finally giving in. "We had a moment last night…"

"Andddd," Lizzie says impatiently.

"We got stuck in the maze when the lights went out. We talked about the kiss, and he said he didn't regret it. But then…" I say, purposely dragging it out to see what Lizzie will say.

"Mills, I love you, but I swear on all things holy if you don't spit it out, I'll—" she starts, and before she can say anything else, I cave.

"He told me he didn't want to push anything because of the inn, so if I wanted him, I was gonna have to beg," I blurt, and I'm met with silence on the other end of the line. "Lizzie, are you still there?"

"Bitch, then what the hell are you doing talking to me instead of asking him to fuck you till you can't walk straight?" she yells.

I can't contain my laughter at her outburst. "Liz!" I scold.

"Sis, I'm sorry. I know you've been out of the dating scene for a while, but this is where you get on your knees and go for it. I mean, really, how does it feel to be God's favorite?"

"Lizzie. This is serious," I yell, shaking my head at her response as I rise from the bed and make my way into the kitchen for my coffee.

"Trust me, Mills, I know. Do you know how many horrible first dates I've been on? Things like this don't just happen. On the last date I went on, the guy insisted he wanted to pay for dinner. Afterward, we went out and had a good time but at the end of the night I refused to sleep with him. Millie, I shit you not, he tried to mail me an itemized bill for what I cost him since

I wouldn't put out… So basically, you have to go for him," Lizzie encourages.

"I know, I know… I'm going crazy here, Liz. But also, I'm terrified. There are so many ways this could go bad," I confess.

My sister lets out a sigh on the other end of the line before saying softly, "I know, but you can't let that fear stop you from going after him, if it's what you want."

"But what if he leaves me? Decides one day that I'm not good enough like Allen did. Think about it… One moment, and ten years were gone just like that. Don't get me wrong, I can see now that we were never right for each other, and I'm absolutely not sad to be divorced from him, but I don't know if I can do it again, Lizzie."

"Oh, Mills…" my sister says, her voice softening at my confession. "First of all, do you really think that you can compare Allen the Asshole to this whole situation? I know I haven't met Brian in person, but from what you've said the two couldn't be more different if they tried. And I love you sis, but that cheating bastard took the last ten years of your life…are you really gonna give him any more control over your happiness? If you ask me, it's time you choose yourself, whatever that looks like."

I pause for a moment, realizing she's right. I haven't been selfish or done anything just because I wanted to in over a decade. All my decisions in my old marriage were made to keep the peace, when I was even given a decision in the first place. I've sacrificed so much of myself, without ever stopping to think what I actually want. If I'm honest, I want to pursue whatever's building with Brian. There's no guarantee that it won't end in disaster, but if I don't let myself go for it, I have a feeling I'll never forgive myself. And despite the fact that I've only known Brian for a few weeks, I know that he would never treat me the way my ex-husband did.

"You're right, sis. I'm sorry, I just don't want to screw this up," I tell her as I take the to-go cup out of the microwave and sip my latte.

"Mills, I'm pretty sure the only thing you should be worried about screwing is that boss of yours," she teases, back to her usual demeanor.

"Okay, okay, I get it!" I say with a laugh.

"All right, sis, I'm about to pass out, but you better keep me updated. Now, go ride 'em cowgirl, or whatever they say down there," she teases.

"Yes, ma'am. Love you big," I tell her, with a laugh.

"Love you bigger, Mils," she replies.

As I end the call and sit in the empty living room, I have to admit that I'm already feeling more at ease. Lizzie's right: if I want a chance at exploring things with Brian, I'm gonna have to go for it.

"So, Millie, the mayor here doesn't have you working too hard, does he?" Huey asks later that night as we finish dinner.

I let out a laugh at the question before looking across the table where Brian's sitting. He's currently running his fingers across my knee under the table, and I feel like I'm seconds away from losing it and begging him to kiss me again, despite the fact we aren't alone right now. Dragging myself out of my daydreams, I pretend to consider my response for a few seconds before saying, "Hmm, I guess he's been all right."

Huey laughs at that, before saying, "Well, girl, you try to keep him in line."

Huey opens his mouth to ask something else when his phone rings. "Hello...yeah... Are you sure? Okay, yes, ma'am, I'll be there in just a minute... Yes, ma'am. See you then," he says to whoever's on the other line before looking at us apologetically.

"Sorry, y'all. That was Miss Agnes. Apparently, she's having some trouble with her shower, and the damned thing is spraying water everywhere. She needs me to come by and give her a hand. I'm sorry to have to run, but I'm gonna have to cut tonight short, I'm afraid," he admits, already standing from his seat.

"Oh, it's no problem," I tell him, grabbing our plates and starting to clean the table.

"Yeah, none at all. Do you need any help?" Brian asks Huey as he shrugs on his jacket.

"No, I'm sure it won't be anything too time consuming, but I appreciate the offer. Y'all just leave the mess, and I'll take care of it when I come home," he says, moving toward the door before stopping. "Damn it, I just realized I haven't fed the cows yet. I've got the buckets of feed ready to go, but I ran out of time to throw them in the trough. Would y'all mind dumping 'em when you head out?

"Sure, that's no problem. I was hoping to get to see them again anyway," I reply honestly as Brian and I move to follow him out. "Thank you again for dinner."

"Of course, y'all don't be strangers, ya' hear?" Huey calls out over his shoulder, already halfway to his truck.

As he pulls out the driveway, I turn to Brian before saying, "All righty then, let's do it."

Damn it, that didn't come out right.

"Thought you'd never ask," he teases, and I try to ignore the smirk on his face at my comment while he steps to the side of the house and grabs the buckets of feed.

His meetings in Saddle Ridge ran longer than planned this afternoon meaning this is the first time we've been alone since last night. I spent the afternoon worrying that it would be awkward, but instead I just feel the desire that seems to be constantly building between us. Each time his hand brushed my arm in the car, or his leg bumped against mine under the dinner table, I became more aware of the way my body was responding to him, and after spending the day thinking about begging for him, I'm desperate for us to be alone and have a chance to talk.

We walk in silence for a moment, carrying the buckets of feed toward the troughs by the gate a couple hundred yards ahead of us. As we walk, his arm bushes mine and I feel the most intense need to feel his hands on me. God, I want him to touch me. The night is dark, the moon hiding behind the clouds and making me squint to see in front of us. The further we get from the house, the harder it is to see, but Brian seems unfazed as he leads us over to the old wooden feeding spot for the cattle.

"Come on," he hollers, rattling the feed around in the bucket. "Dinner time, come on."

All of a sudden, the cows are everywhere, mooing their demands for us to dump the buckets by our feet into the trough on the other side of the gate. After a moment Brian obliges and dumps both of his buckets, and we step back to watch them eat. He's standing so close, all I want to do is reach out and pull him to me, but just as I'm trying to talk myself into going for it, I notice the small calf I fed the last time I was here making her way over. She sticks her head through the metal gate, ignoring the feed and waiting for us to focus our attention on her. Reaching out my hand, I spend a moment rubbing her cold snout, and she lets out a happy moooooo, making me laugh.

"God, it's not fair. Even the animals are obsessed with you," he teases, bumping me gently with his shoulder.

My body heats at the contact, and I resist the urge to lean into him too much before rolling my eyes in his direction.

"So…" he says as I give the calf another pat and turn to face him. "I've barely talked to you today. Did you enjoy your day off?"

"Yes, it was wonderful. I went on a long run and spent the rest of the day watching my favorite Christmas movies," I respond as he reaches out, touching the belt loop on my jeans and tugging me toward him. My breath hitches at the contact, and I take a breath to steady myself before deciding to continue. "I also did a lot of thinking."

"Oh, is that right?" he asks, his tone more serious than before. "About…"

"What you said last night," I continue as he traces his hand through my hair, my nerves building in my stomach at the confession I'm about to make until I feel nauseous.

"Hmm, and what did you decide?" he prompts, both of us unable to look away from the other.

I take a deep breath before looking at him and saying, "Brian Jones, would you please fuck me?"

CHAPTER 15

BRIAN

id she just say what I think she said?

We stare at each other, and I almost laugh at the surprised expression on her face, like she can't believe she allowed herself to say the words out loud. I pause for a moment, waiting to see if she'll change her mind. Then we're moving at the same time, pouncing on each other. Her lips meet mine, and I sink into her hard kiss already desperate to feel all of her.

"Damn it, Millie. Thank God." I groan into her mouth, as I run my hands up and down her sides. "Jesus, I've been thinking about this all day."

"Me too," she says between kisses, pulling me closer to her.

"Come on, we've gotta get out of here. I swear these damn cows are not gonna be watching when I see you naked for the first time," I say, grabbing her hand and leading her back to the truck.

Jumping in the driver's seat, I throw the truck in drive and barrel out of Huey's driveway. I tell myself I need to slow down, but as Millie grazes her hand up and down my arm, I lose all sense of thought.

Finally, after what feels like forever, I pull into the driveway, and before I've shifted it into park I'm reaching and pulling her into my lap, needing to touch her. All night, I've been so close to her, inhaling her vanilla perfume and dreaming about feeling her mouth on mine. Now, after her confession, I feel like I'll combust if I don't get my hands on her.

My mouth meets hers, and I kiss her like a man possessed. Running my mouth down her neck, she lets out a moan that goes straight to my dick, and before we make our way inside, I push her against the front door. Wrapping my hand around the front of her throat, I relish the needy sounds she makes each time I have her in this position and deepen the kiss.

"Brian, please," she whines. I keep her pinned to the door while I fumble through my pocket with my other hand, looking for the key. Finally, after what feels like forever, I pull it out and unlock the door, moving both of us inside. We're barely over the threshold, before I give in and run my hands under Millie's sweater, desperate to feel her smooth skin under me.

"Are you sure this is what you want," I whisper, running my hands gently across her back. *God, it'll kill me if she says no, but I can't resist the need to be sure.*

"You know, I'm usually all about the whole perfect gentleman thing you've got going on, but I swear to fuck, if you don't get me naked in the next two minutes, I'm literally gonna lose my mind."

"Yes, ma'am," I tease, smirking at her enthusiasm before pulling the sweater over her head. "God, these tits are fucking perfect."

She arches her chest into me, and I cup her breasts through the pink lace of her bra before leaning down and teasing her nipple through the fabric.

"Brian," she groans, clawing her hands through my hair and tugging me closer to her.

"What do you want, sweet girl?" I whisper, swapping to her other breast and giving it the same treatment.

"You, please, just touch me," she groans, giving a sharp tug on my hair as I pull down the lacy fabric and graze her nipple with my teeth.

"I told you all you had to do was ask," I taunt, pushing her back until she collapses on the couch behind her. I let my hands drift to the button of her jeans and undo them. After, I pull the zipper down, brushing my fingers across the front of her panties.

Damn it, she's fucking soaked.

The little bit of control I've been desperately clinging to, trying to take this as slow as possible, completely snaps. I grab the tops of her jeans and jerk them down in one smooth motion so that she's completely bare in front of me except for her panties.

"God, you're so damn wet," I tell her, pulling her matching pink panties to the side and running my hand through her slit.

"Please," she begs, "Please just—"

"Br–Br–Bri," she whimpers, as I slide my fingers inside her. *God, she's perfect.*

"I've got you, Mills," I promise before adding a second finger and working them in tandem.

"Oh my God—" she whimpers. "You feel so good."

"Is this all you want," I tease, continuing to play with her pussy, leaning up and pressing a wet kiss to her mouth. Every sound she makes drives me fucking insane, and I don't remember another time I've ever wanted a woman this bad. "Or are you gonna let me taste you?"

She lets out a surprised squeak, scooting her bottom closer to the edge of the cushion. "You—you want to…"

"Uh, yeah, unless you're not into it…" I trail off, continuing to tease her and waiting to see what she'll say.

"Well, I've never really done that," she admits quietly, refusing to make eye contact with me at that confession.

Wait, what? Did she just say what I think she said?

"Millie, are you telling me that no one has ever tasted your sweet pussy?" I growl, reaching my other hand up to grab her chin, forcing her eyes to meet mine.

She shakes her head, still looking embarrassed.

"Come on, don't get shy on me now," I insist, continuing to pump my fingers in and out of her, letting my hand bump against her clit as I try to bring her focus back to me. "Use your words, Mills, and tell me you want my mouth on you. I've been dreaming about you wrapping your thighs around my face and letting me taste how bad you want me to fuck you."

I pause for a moment, holding my breath to see what she'll say.

"Brian, please," she whispers, and I feel a smirk spread across my face.

"Such a good girl," I murmur, pulling my hand from where I've been teasing her. She cries out at the loss of contact, and I smile at her reaction. "Hmm, someone's feeling a little needy, huh?" I tease before reaching up and slowly pulling her panties down her legs. As I trace them further and further, I lean over and start trailing kisses up her thigh. "It's okay, Mills, I'm gonna take care of you."

The closer I get to her center, the more she writhes beneath me, rolling her hips to try to pull my body into hers. I inch closer before blowing a burst of cool air across her pussy, loving the way she responds to my teasing, before I finally give in. When I flick my tongue across her center, she lets out a yelp, wrapping one of her legs around my shoulder and using that leverage to grind against my face.

"God, yes," she says as I begin to work my hand in tandem with my tongue, already feeling her make her way towards her release. I spend several minutes teasing her, pulling back when I can tell she's getting close.

"Millie, you taste so good," I murmur, before leaning back in and grazing my teeth across her clit. She lets out a loud yelp before wrapping both legs around me and pulling me to her. I try to take my time tasting her, but I can tell she's racing toward an orgasm, and honestly, I can't wait to feel her come on my fingers and mouth. Deciding to give her what she wants, I start moving my hand faster. She rolls her hips, finding a rhythm, fucking my fingers and mouth until she cries out, coming hard.

I pull back, sitting on my heels in front of the sofa where she's spread out before me, giving her a moment to catch her breath. After a moment, she smiles before saying, "That was incredible."

"Yeah, I couldn't agree more," I tell her, as she grabs my hand and pulls me closer to her. She kisses me, tentatively at first, but deepening the kiss after a moment.

"You like tasting yourself on me, Millie? You taste so damn sweet," I tell her, trying to ignore the way she's pressing herself against my still covered cock.

"Mm hmm, but now I want to feel you inside me," she whispers, rolling her hips once and I feel my dick twitch in my jeans.

"That can be arranged," I reply. Reaching down, I push my boxers down my legs, unable to wait any longer. I free my cock and take it in my hand, teasing her with it. *Shit, she feels so good.*

"Hold on. Let me grab a condom," I groan, hating the idea of leaving her spread on the couch to spend the next few minutes digging through my bedside drawer instead of feeling her wrapped around me.

"Don't," she whispers. "I've had an IUD for years, and I got tested as soon as I found out about—"

"Millie, I swear, if I hear you say another man's name while you're naked in my house, begging for my cock, I will not be held responsible for my actions," I growl, reaching down and swatting at her ass.

"Yes, sir," she whispers, and just like every other time I've heard her say those words, I have to fight the growl that wants to work out of my lips. "I'm sorry. I just mean, unless you have an objection, I want to feel you bare."

Damn it, this woman is gonna be the death of me.

"No objections here," I mutter, before dropping another kiss on her mouth. She kisses me eagerly as I line myself up with her entrance and pause, making sure she hasn't changed her mind.

Instead, she wraps her leg around my back and pulls me closer, helping me slide into her tight pussy. I'm barely halfway in, trying to fight the urge to slam into her when she moans. "God, you're so damn big."

I kiss her again as I inch in a bit more, giving her time to adjust and reaching down to flick her clit with my hand. It's been years since I took a woman like this, and never without a condom. The combination has me feeling completely wild for her, and it's all I can do to resist pinning her down against the cushions and fucking her like a man possessed.

"You can take me, baby. Shit, your pussy is so fucking tight," I say, continuing to ease in while I play with her until I'm fully inside her.

I give her another moment to adjust until she starts rolling her hips against me. "Okay, please move. Jesus, I need to feel you."

Thank fuck, I think, pulling back slowly and pushing back into her hard. She lets out a loud cry as I slide in and out of her a few more times, before she begs, "Faster, please. Please, go faster."

After that, I let my need for her take over, fucking her hard. Her tits bounce in front of me as I continue to play with her clit, and I know I need to get her there fast because there's no way I can keep this up.

"Come on, Mills. I need to feel this sweet pussy coming around my cock," I growl, and after a few more moments I feel her start to clench around me. "Shit, you're so damn perfect."

She comes with a cry, and as soon as I can feel her orgasm, I grab her hips and fuck her hard. Feeling the way she grips my cock as she comes triggers my own release, and I let out a growl as I fill her with my cum.

Stilling my hips, we lie there for a moment, both trying to catch our breath. After a few minutes, Millie leans over and drops a kiss on my lips before breaking the silence. "Damn. That was…"

"Fucking incredible," I tell her, wrapping my arm around her and holding her to my chest.

"Pretty much," she answers, nuzzling her head into me and making herself comfortable. A part of me knows we should probably get up and take a shower, but having her in my arms after what we just shared feels right.

I kiss her forehead, and as we both sit there clinging to each other, I can't help but wonder how I'll ever let her go.

CHAPTER 16
MILLIE

"Good morning, beautiful." I hear just as a pair of lips brush my forehead. "I know we had a long night, but we've gotta get moving."

Groaning, I open my eyes to see Brian fully dressed, waiting for me to drag myself out of bed. When I check my phone, I'm surprised to see that it's barely after seven. *Damn, I'm exhausted.*

After the most incredible sex of my life last night, Brian pulled me into the shower and continued his teasing touches while he washed my body. By the time he pushed me against the wall and slid inside me, I was begging him to take me again.

"Umm, do we have something that I've forgotten about?" I asked, throwing my arm over my eyes.

"Nope, but come on, I have a surprise for you," he says, pulling back my arm and giving me an animated smile. While I'm usually not a morning person, the excitement on his face is obvious, so I pull myself out of the bed and hurry to get ready.

"Okay… Where are we going?" I ask, looking through my clothes for something to wear.

"Mills, come on. What part of 'surprise' do you not understand?" he teases.

"All right, fine… Gimme ten minutes to get ready," I

respond, grabbing an emerald-green sweater and my favorite pair of jeans.

Throwing on my clothes, I spend a few minutes putting on makeup and running my brush through my knotted hair.

"All right, I'm ready when you are," I call out so that Brian can hear me in the kitchen before grabbing my cell and heading out of my room.

"Perfect, come on then," he says as I exit my room and see him sitting at his kitchen island. "I fixed you a cup of coffee. Grab it if you want it on the way out."

"Bless you," I tease with a laugh, walking over and taking a large sip out of the blue to-go cup he's made a habit of fixing for me every morning.

When I first moved in, I worried living with Brian would feel too similar to the penthouse I shared with Allen for the last decade— full of passive aggressive silence and never-ending chores thanks to my ex-husband's unrealistic standards. Instead, living with Brian has been surprisingly fun, and he's constantly doing little things to show he's thinking about me, like making my morning coffee and slipping a gallon of chocolate ice cream in the freezer after I mentioned I'd been craving something sweet.

After last night, I'd been briefly concerned that sleeping with him would ruin the easygoing roommate routine we had going, but I should have known better.

"We'll be outside for a bit this morning, so you'll probably need your jacket," he says, gesturing to the chair where he threw my jacket last night in his hurry to get me undressed.

"Okay, but can I at least get a hint?" I tease, poking out my lip like I'm pouting.

Immediately, he leans over and sucks my bottom lip into his mouth, kissing me hard enough to leave me breathless. Reaching my arms around his neck, I let out a surprised whimper and melt further into the kiss as one hand pulls me closer and the other wraps around my neck, teasing me slightly and making me moan.

"Damn it, Millie," he groans, pulling back and pressing his forehead against mine. "I could kiss you all day, but if we don't get going, I'm gonna end up keeping you hostage in bed. And as good as that sounds, I really want to take you somewhere."

"I wouldn't mind that," I whisper, leaning back in to kiss him again.

He places a light kiss on my mouth before pulling back again, giving me a look of frustration. "Millie, you're killing me. Please, let me surprise you."

I can't help but laugh at the tortured expression on his face. "Fine, fine… I'll be good. But we better get out of here fast before either of us changes our mind."

"Yep, you're right. Let's go," he says, gesturing for me to lead the way.

We walk to his truck in silence, and it takes way more willpower than I'd like to admit to resist reaching for him again.

After jumping in the truck, Brian fiddles with the radio for a second before finding the station of Christmas classics and pulling out of the driveway. I have to fight the urge to ask him again where we're going, but since he seems determined for it to be a surprise, I decide to distract myself by singing loudly to the radio.

I hit a few particularly bad notes, and Brian chuckles, screwing his nose in an overly exaggerated wince at the sound of my singing.

I open my mouth to say something else when the truck slows to a stop. I look out the window to figure out where we are, to see Brian pulling into the parking lot of Coopers'. I shoot him a confused look. "Okayyy, I'm lost. What are we doing here?'

"Well, I remembered what you said about your ex-husband never wanting any Christmas decorations, and then I thought about how damn hard you've been working at the inn, and I just felt like I needed to do something. So, I thought I would surprise you with a Christmas tree, but if you don't want it…" he starts, but before he can finish, I'm launching myself across the seat and kissing him again.

God, could this man be any more perfect?

I pull away a moment later, squeezing his hand in mine. "Brian, this is perfect. Oh my gosh, I haven't had a tree in over ten years. Can I decorate it too?"

He shoots me a wide smile before saying, "Of course, Mills. Yesterday when I was in Saddle Ridge, I ran into that store you liked and grabbed all the pink decorations they had. You know the ones you wanted for the inn but wouldn't get because you thought Deer Valley's needed to be more traditional?"

I stare at him for a moment, unable to believe he did all this for me. "Brian, I can't believe you did all this… I just…" I stammer, feeling off kilter by the whole encounter. I truly don't remember a time that someone did something this nice for me.

After a moment, Brian realizes he's rendered me speechless, and he leans over and kisses me softly on the lips. "Millie Pouncey, you'd better never forget that you are worthy of someone who treats you like you're not an inconvenience or an afterthought, because that's the furthest thing from the truth. Now, let's go get you that tree."

I smile at him, feeling myself falling for him a little more with every confession like that he gives me. God, I really think I love this man.

Wait, what? The thought hits me out of nowhere, making my nerves rise for a moment. After everything that happened in D.C., I can't help but feel anxious at the thought of giving my heart to someone else so soon, especially someone I've only known for a month. But at the same time, it only took me days to realize that Brian couldn't be any more different than my ex-husband if he tried. While Allen looked for ways to control me and make sure I always felt inferior to him, Brian builds me up and makes me feel invincible. As scary as it is to think about how this could end, I refuse to let myself pass up someone who makes me so incredibly happy.

It feels like a weight is lifted as he opens my door, and we walk through the entrance of the tree farm. It's still before eight on a Saturday morning, so I'm not surprised that the farm is mostly empty other than the cashier working the front register and the attendants cutting down the trees selected for purchase. As we walk, Brian threads his fingers through mine, pulling me closer to him.

"I'm shocked we haven't seen a soul you know," I tease him before continuing. "Is it just me waiting for one of the nosey locals to pop out between the trees with a camera? Oh my gosh, imagine what would happen if they saw us like this."

"Well, I could think of worse things, I reckon," he says with a wink. "Honestly Millie, I'm not gonna hide how attracted I am to you unless you ask me to. But we've got a busy few days getting ready for the gala and I want us to be able to figure out whatever this is between us without all their bullshit. What do you think?"

"Hmm, I think you just don't want to lose your title of Most Eligible Bachelor, Mr. Mayor," I taunt playfully, bumping him with my shoulder as we continue walking through the trees.

He rolls his eyes at me before saying sarcastically, "Yeah, I'm sure that's it."

"Speaking of which, I know you told me you never brought women home because of Miss Ethel, and you haven't seriously dated anyone because you were taking care of everyone else, but how in the hell did you keep the women you went out with or hooked up with a secret in this place?" I ask, my tone light, but genuinely curious.

Brian looks down and quirks his brow at my question. "Millie, I think you misunderstood. It's not that I just didn't have a girlfriend or bring women home. When I was first elected, Miss Agnes pressured me into going out with her granddaughter. By the time we finished our drinks, there were rumors I was going to propose. On top of everything else, I just didn't have time to deal with it. So, I haven't done it in years."

My jaw drops at his admission. I knew he said his dad getting sick had changed his priorities, but I figured he'd still had flings with women. "Wait, so you mean to tell me that last night…"

"Yeah. I thought you understood. First time in years."

I open my mouth to reply, but can't think of an intelligent response before he continues, "Mills, let me be clear. This thing with us isn't casual for me. Yes, the sex was incredible, but I'm not looking for a casual hookup. I know we haven't known each other that long, and you've got a lot going on. So why don't we just take this slow and see where it goes. We can talk about it after the holidays."

"Uhh, oh… okay," I say, still feeling the shock of his confession and trying to ignore the effect it has on me. I knew last night wasn't something he regularly did but hearing him share a lot of what I've been feeling has me feeling giddy.

"Sooo…back to this Christmas tree. What do you think about that one?" he asks, pointing to a large eight-foot tree to our right.

"It's perfect," I say, unable to stop the smile from spreading across my face. "You really didn't have to do this."

"I know, Mills, but I wanted to," he says with a wink.

He motions the attendant over and before I know it, we're making our way back to the truck with our new tree in tow.

"Before we head home, I've gotta grab some paperwork from my office in City Hall. It shouldn't take more than a few minutes," he tells me as he pulls out of the parking lot.

"Oh, sure. That's no problem," I tell him, turning my phone over in the cupholder where I left it earlier. I chuckle to myself when I see some messages from my sister.

> Lizzie: Okay, I was trying to be patient, but we both know that's never been my strong suit.

Lizzie: Please tell me you and that boss of
yours are fa la la fucking right now…

Lizzie: COME ON MILLS! I NEED TO KNOW!

Shaking my head at her antics, I debate making her wait before telling her the truth, but gosh I need to talk to someone about all of this.

"I'll be right back," Brian says, and I look up to realize we're already parked in front of City Hall.

He leans over and kisses me before jumping out, and I turn back to my phone, typing.

Me: Ummmmm…

Lizzie: Bitch I swear to God if you don't spill…

Me: We slept together last night…

Me: Liz, it was fucking incredible.

Me: And then he woke me up this morning and took me to pick out a Christmas tree since I mentioned when I got here that Allen never let me decorate.

Me: And last but not least, he told me that I'm the first woman he's hooked up with in YEARS…

Lizzie: SIS…

Lizzie: I mean this in the most respectful way possible…

Lizzie: If you don't fucking marry that man, I will.

Lizzie: Okay, not really, you know I'm more of a city girl. But really, OH MY GOD!!!

Lizzie: There's a lot here to unpack…

As I read her texts, I finally try to make sense of the events over the last twenty-four hours. Everything has been incredible, but I still don't really know what we're doing. I know Brian said he was serious, but what does that look like? And for how long? He said we would talk after the holidays, so he could be planning to try to let me down easy after the gala. Here I am thinking I'm in love with him, but what if he's just being nice to make sure I don't leave before the events are finished.

Me: TELL ME ABOUT IT.

Me: I like him so much, but what if he decides it's not worth the trouble after the holidays. He said we would talk after Christmas, but we haven't even discussed if Deer Valley Inn wants to keep me on after the gala.

Me: I feel like we're living in a fantasy right now, and I don't know what I'll do if he comes to his senses and ends things. I mean, he's my boss and we're living together...

Lizzie: Nope.

Lizzie: I love you sis, but we aren't doing this.

Lizzie: Do you really think a man is gonna go six years without any on top of doing all this lover boy shit, which you totally deserve by the way, just to send you packing in a week's time. I think the fuck not.

Lizzie: There are times for us to be delusional, but this is not one of them ma'am.

Lizzie: Just try not to think too hard about it and enjoy the time with him. We'll worry about what comes next when we get there.

I smile at her text, feeling myself start to calm down a bit. The more I think about it, I have to admit she's probably right. And even if Brian decides he doesn't want me to stay, it won't be the first time I have to start over. So really, what's the harm in enjoying some earth-shattering orgasms in the meantime.

Me: I guess you're right.

Lizzie: Of course I am *eye roll*

Me: Gah, you're so humble...

Lizzie: Yeah, yeah. Anyway, back to the important stuff. So... the sex... Tell me everything.

Lizzie: Please tell me Mr. Mayor finally gave you an orgasm... or three...

Me: More like four...

Lizzie: HELL YES!

Lizzie: Christmas miracles really do exist!

Lizzie: Damn it, I've gotta get back to this sketch I'm working on. It's gotta be done before I leave for Christmas and I'm really not sure I can get it done in the next three days. But really sis, don't forget you deserve to be happy, and fuck anyone or anything that tells you otherwise.

I feel my throat clog at the sincerity of her text. Damn it, I've missed her pep talks over the last few years.

Me: Love you big, sis.

Lizzie: Love you bigger Mills, and don't you forget it.

I throw my phone back in the cupholder just as Brian returns to the truck with a stack of papers folded into a notebook. He jumps in the front seat and leans over, kissing me quickly before he pulls back and throws the truck in reverse.

"Ready to head home and decorate that tree?" he asks, placing his hand over mine, and rubbing my knuckles with his fingertips.

And in that moment, I realize Brian's house has become more of a home than the cold and uninviting penthouse I shared with Allen ever was. My sister's right. I'm gonna soak in every moment, every kiss, and every earth-shattering orgasm and worry about the rest later.

I lean over and press a kiss to Brian's temple, before saying, "Yep, let's get ready to deck the halls."

CHAPTER 17

BRIAN

"Yes, ma'am… Yep, we can do that… All righty, yes, ma'am, we'll see y'all then," Millie says, before putting her phone away and ending the call with a frustrated groan.

"Oh my gosh, I swear every time I think I've answered all of Miss Sally's questions, she finds another reason to call me," she says, rubbing her face with her hand.

"Join the club," I say with a grimace.

"Okay, I'm pausing for coffee. I'll be right back," she says, standing from her chair, and making her way out the door of my office, where we've spent the entire day working. Millie's been wrapped up with calls for the Gingerbread Gala, and I took the day off from my mayoral duties to catch up at Deer Valley. I told myself that my reasons for making that decision were purely work related, but a larger part of me wanted to spend more time with Millie after the weekend we shared.

Before Millie, weekends were for volunteering with some of the various committees I serve on, filling in at the inn, and occasionally grabbing a beer with a couple of the guys like Will from the high school. But after we picked out the tree on Saturday, Millie put me to work helping her decorate, working her magic on the eight-foot tree until every inch was covered in lights and pastel ornaments. Yesterday, I briefly considered coming into work to give her some space, not wanting Millie to feel suffocated after living and working with me for the last several weeks. Instead, she suggested a *Home Alone* marathon, and we'd settled in on the couch in front of the tree. We spent the majority of the day tangled up, kissing and teasing each other until we finally gave in. I've gotta say, after fucking her in the glow of the lights, I've never been more in the Christmas spirit.

The rational part of my brain keeps telling myself I need to slow this down between us. Not because I want to, but I'm scared if we move too fast, I'll run her off. At the same time, I can't seem to help myself when I'm around her.

The door opens again, and Millie walks in carrying two cups of coffee. "Here you go. I've still got a ton of work to do, so it looks like we're in for a long night."

"Thanks," I tell her, taking the cup and trying to hide my grimace at the cinnamon aroma I can already tell is coming out of the cup.

Damn it, I really fucking hate cinnamon.

Taking a few sips of the offending liquid, I gesture to the desk where Millie has been working. "You know, at this time of night, I think we could have gone for a glass of wine instead."

She takes a long drink of her latte before answering. "I definitely thought about it, but the line for the restaurant is out the door. There literally hasn't been a day since I got here that they weren't wrapped up."

"Yeah, I'm excited to see the numbers from this quarter. Between all the guests we've had and that magazine write up, we've never been this busy."

"That's great," Millie says, throwing herself into her chair and turning back to her notes.

"So, how's it coming over here?" I ask, leaning in toward her.

Millie runs her hands through her hair and groans. "I feel like I'm never gonna get everything done. I know I've done this a hundred times, but I've always had a team of people making sure everything runs smoothly. And bless Miss Ethel and some of the other ladies, but every time I try to ask them something, they get distracted and start asking me questions."

Chucking at her frustration, I reach out and push a piece of hair behind her ear. "Oh Mills, I don't believe that for a minute. Well, except for your volunteers being nosey. That I completely believe. But really, you don't have anything to worry about. I've seen all your plans, and they're fucking incredible."

She smiles at that, and I can't resist the urge to pull her to me. As soon as I'm close enough, I reach down and kiss her. I've barely touched my lips to hers when I remember where I am. *Damn it. I swore I wouldn't take advantage of being her boss.* I can't explain why kissing her at home is any different than in the office, but all my hesitation from before surges back at the thought of her feeling like I'm taking advantage of the situation.

Shit, if she decides I'm using her job to pressure her, she could leave after the gala. I know I told her I was interested in seeing where this goes, but she didn't really say anything else. If I run her off like that, I'll never forgive myself.

Millie must register the change in my demeanor because she looks up at me with confusion on her face.

"We can't," I tell her, trying to restrain myself from pinning her to my desk and tasting her sweet pussy. *Fuck, some kind of boss I am.*

"Oh, uh sorry," she mumbles. "I, uhh—I'm sorry."

She starts to nervously rifle through the papers when several of them scatter to the floor. "Damn it," she mutters, sinking to her knees. "I just can't do anything right tonight," she whispers miserably.

Fuck it. There's no way I can watch this girl think I don't want her, professionalism be damned. Reaching down, I pull her up until she's standing in front of me.

"Millie Pouncey, you're driving me wild, do you know that? Here I am, trying to be good while we're at work, but all day all

I've been able to think about is how incredible you would look bent over my desk. I told myself I could wait until we were done here, but dang if you didn't destroy every bit of self-control I had with one kiss."

"I'm sorry," she whispers, not looking the least bit apologetic. "But I heard a rumor that professionalism is overrated."

"Amen," I tease, before crossing the room and turning the lock on the door. Turning back, I pull her close again and kiss her hard. She responds immediately, tracing her fingers through my hair and tugging me to her like she's scared that if she doesn't, I'll pull away.

That motion snaps the tiny bit of control I was struggling to hold onto. I reach down and I grab her legs, hitching them both around my waist and carrying her over to my desk while I kiss her hard.

"If you don't want this, you better tell me now, Miss Pouncey," I growl, running my hands up to cup her tits through her sweater.

"Please, Brian, fuck me, please," she cries out, and I smile at her response.

"Well, you know how much I like it when you beg," I murmur, unbuttoning her jeans and pulling them along with her panties down quickly. God, I can't wait to be inside her again. I keep one hand on her, running my finger across her clit to tease her as I unbutton my jeans. I'd planned on teasing her for a few minutes to make sure she was ready to take my cock, but I can already tell she's soaked again.

"Hold on, baby, I need to feel you," I tell her, lining myself up with her entrance and pushing into her hard.

She lets out a high-pitched whimper, locking her legs around me and leaning back on her forearms against my desk. Watching her expression as I slam into her has me edging toward a release faster than I'd like but damn she's so fucking sexy. Reaching down between us, I toy with her clit, desperate for her to get there before I do.

"Damn, you're so beautiful when you're taking my cock," I tell her, pinching my fingers together and feeling her pussy contract.

"Don't stop," she begs, and I feel her legs that are wrapped around me start to shake.

"Come for me, Millie," I respond, continuing to push in and out of her until she lets out a nearly silent scream. As soon as I feel her start to come, I give in and find my release with her. I'm pretty sure I let out a groan as I pour into her, but I'm not sure, only able to focus on how incredible she feels.

"Shit, you're perfect," I say, dropping a kiss on her mouth before pulling out and watching my release start to leak out of her. "Damn, that's so fucking sexy."

Millie just smiles in agreement, and I lean down to grab her pants off the floor. I'd love to stay cooped up in this office just like this, alternating between working and having more incredible sex, but I know that there's a ton of work to do before the Gingerbread Gala. Reluctantly, I help her pull her pants up her legs before pulling her in close and running my lips down her neck.

"All right, Miss Pouncey, we need to get back to work, but I want you to remember as you make phone calls and check things off your to-do list that it's my cum dripping out of your sweet pussy. And when we get home tonight, you're all mine. Do you understand?"

She looks up at me, and it's impossible to miss the desire in her eyes. After a moment of staring into her heated gaze, she nods and murmurs "Yes, sir," before standing and shooting a wink in my direction.

Yep. I'm sure I'll be getting tons of "work" done tonight.

THE FOLLOWING MORNING I'M TRYING TO REPLY TO SOME EMAILS IN the kitchen while I wait for Millie to return from her run. But instead of focusing on budget reports and the minutes from the latest city council meeting, I'm plagued with one thought... *Damn it, I've totally fallen for this girl.*

Last night, like every other time I've had sex with Millie, was absolutely incredible. I can still picture the way she begged me to fuck her. I'm pretty sure I'll be dreaming about the look she had as I thrusted into her and made her scream for the foreseeable future. When we got home from the inn, she asked me to shower with her, and I soaked in every moment of being able to reach out and touch her smooth skin. Finally, after pressing her against the shower wall and feeling her come apart on my face and then my cock, we collapsed into my bed together. I love waking up with her wrapped around me.

But as much as I love having her here, and I can't deny that I'm completely gone for her, there's a nagging part of my brain that keeps reminding me we're running out of time.

Thanks to the arrangement we made, there's nothing tying her to me after the Gingerbread Gala. She could pack up and be gone before it's time to take the decorations down. I've completely failed at taking this slow, and for all I know, she could be planning her escape from this little town as we speak. Her insurance finalized her claim this week, and I'm pretty sure she'll have a check for her totaled vehicle in the next few days. After that, there's really nothing holding her here.

God, I want her to stay. But at the same time, can I really expect someone as incredible as Millie to commit to staying in Springside after the last three weeks?

Blowing out a breath, I try to refocus myself on the work in front of me, just as she comes in the door.

"Good morning," she says with a smile, before bending down and untying her shoes. "Sorry if I'm a little later than normal. I kind of got in the zone and didn't realize how far I'd gone until it was too late."

"No problem. How far'd you go this morning?" I ask, taking a sip of my vanilla flavored coffee. *No cinnamon in sight this morning, thank fuck.*

"I got about five miles. I only planned to do three, but I guess I had a lot on my mind with the gala coming up tomorrow," she apologizes as she sits her running shoes by the door and plugs up the headphones she wears each morning during her workouts.

Hmm, that makes two of us, I think, as I watch her go through her morning rituals, and I try not to dwell on how easily we've settled into a routine together. She grabs a bottle of water, before turning with a smile and saying, "Let me take a quick shower, and I'll be ready to go. I've got a big day today trying to get everything decorated."

"No problem, I've cleared the day to help with whatever you need," I tell her, closing my computer and walking over to kiss her softly.

"Oh, wow, thanks, Brian. You didn't have to do that, but I can't say I won't put you to work," she teases with a laugh.

"Sure. Surprisingly, December 23rd isn't a big day at City Hall anyway," I respond before refilling my coffee cup and filling her usual to-go cup at the same time.

"Well thanks anyway," she says. "Give me about fifteen and I'll be ready."

With that, she turns and heads down the hall, and I blow out a breath. *Why is it so freaking easy to be around her, but so damn hard to ask her to stay?*

CHAPTER 18

MILLIE

Christmas Eve has always been one of my favorite days. The anticipation of what's coming the next day makes everything feel magical, like even the air knows something special is coming. But I never realized how magnified that feeling could be surrounded by hundreds of other people.

I've spent the entire day running around like crazy. Between making sure the band and the photographers have everything that they need, ensuring the wine from the winery is fully stocked, checking in with the kitchen staff on the status of the food, and fielding the questions from all the volunteers, I'm already dreaming about getting in the bed. But instead, I'm in Brian's office touching up my makeup and throwing on my gown for the night.

When I told Lizzie about the event, she'd insisted on finding the perfect dress for me, and since I didn't happen to pack any evening gowns when I fled the city, I didn't see any reason to turn her down. But last night, when I opened the package and saw the most beautiful dress I've ever seen in my life, I squealed. The emerald-green makes my eyes sparkle, and the way the fabric dips and pulls makes my curves look incredible.

A knock comes from the door, and I call out, "You can come

in," as I put my long silver earrings in and glance at the mirror. I watch Brian enter his office through the reflection, and even if I wasn't wearing the most perfect dress known to man, the look on his face would have made me feel like the most beautiful girl in the world.

"Wow, Mills, you look…" he says, trailing off as he stares at me. "God, you look perfect."

I blush at his admission and smooth the fabric down over my legs. "Thank you. You know I had to find something worthy of being on your arm, Mr. Mayor," I tease, and he lets out a laugh at my dramatics before giving me a serious look.

"Yeah, whatever. I can't wait to get you home and get you out of that dress," he murmurs before dropping a kiss on my lips. I lean into him, but before I can deepen the kiss, he brushes his hand through my hair and continues. "We both know that you're the one this town's obsessed with. But really, you know you're more than worthy, right? You're magnificent, Mills," he says, and I'm about to argue with him when I recognize the sincerity in his voice.

I smile, and all of a sudden, I'm hit with how quickly Brian's worked his way into my heart. I may have spent the last ten years married and attending events like this at least once a week, but the last few days have been the first time I've truly felt beautiful and valued. Not only that, but Brian treats me like an equal instead of a servant or an inconvenience. It also doesn't hurt the way he fucks me like I'm a queen.

He holds out his arm for me to take before saying, "All right, enough of that, you've worked your tail off for this event, and people will start arriving soon. Let's go celebrate!"

Wrapping my arm in his, we exit the office where the entire first floor has been completely transformed. Each wall is decorated with gingerbread decor, making the room resemble the inside of a gingerbread house. The wall behind the band will sparkle with hundreds of lights that we spent several hours hanging yesterday, making the room feel like a magical wonder-land as soon as we plug them in.

"I'll be right back," Brian whispers as we stand admiring the room before us. "I just need to take care of the lights."

He leaves, and a minute later the curtain of lights starts to shimmer as he lowers the flood lights in the lobby. As I wait for him to make his way back over, Bridget walks through the door and immediately heads in my direction.

"Millie, this is incredible," she says as she wraps her arm around my shoulder, pulling me into a hug. "After seeing what you did with the maze, I knew this would be good, but it's better than anything we've ever had here in Springside. When I came in this morning, I literally couldn't believe how much you trans-formed this place in less than twenty-four hours."

I smile at her compliment, before responding. "Thanks, Brid-get. I couldn't have done it without Brian though."

Bridget gives me a skeptical look. "Brian? Like my cousin Brian? He doesn't have much of an eye for design."

I let out a laugh at her statement. "No? Well, maybe not, but he really was great."

"Well, I'm glad to hear it. You've been just what we needed around here. Please tell me you're planning to stay after the holi-days," she insists.

"Oh, uh, well," I stammer. "I…I don't know."

"Well, where else would you go?" she asks. "Or are we too small for ya?"

"No, not at all. I just need to talk to Brian and make sure the offer still stands. He hasn't mentioned anything about what would happen after tonight," I admit sheepishly.

"God, for someone so smart, he really is a dumb ass," she groans, throwing her hands up in frustration. "Millie, that man is obsessed with you. He may not have said it, but there's no way he doesn't want you to stay. Just promise me you won't leave until you talk to him, especially if you really do want to stay."

"I promise," I say, blowing out a breath.

"What are you promising?" Brian asks as he rejoins us in the center of the room. Guests are starting to arrive, and I'd be lying if I said I wasn't a little excited to see their reaction to the work we'd done over the last few weeks.

"Oh, I was just making Millie promise to finally go out to karaoke with me now that her asshole boss doesn't have her working all hours of the day," Bridget teases, winking in my direction as she delivers the fib.

"Her words, not mine," I say, not wanting Brian to think I'm complaining about work.

"Well, I've just gotta say, I've heard both of y'all sing, and I send my condolences to the other patrons of Maracas," he pokes back, causing Bridget and I both to chuckle. He's not exactly wrong.

We chat for a few minutes as people continue entering. Eventually, Miss Ethel makes her way over, waving her hand toward the decor.

"Millie, how on earth did you pull all of this off?" she asks, gesturing to the lights where the band is starting to play.

"Oh, I just had lots of fabulous help," I respond, smiling at the group of ladies that seems to accumulate whenever Miss Ethel starts asking questions.

Miss Agnes steps up before asking, "Dear, please tell me we get to look forward to lots of these in the future."

I smile at her compliment before shrugging. "I definitely have enjoyed planning these." I'm deflecting but until I have time to talk to Brian, I'm not exactly sure how to respond.

"Well, I think if our mayor here isn't smart enough to figure out how to keep you in town, he isn't as cut out for this job as we like to think he is," Miss Ethel says.

"I agree," Miss Agnes says, just as Miss Sally makes her way over to us.

"Hmm, well I think y'all are all a bunch of idiots," she calls out, hitting me with her signature look of disdain. "We'll be getting those real estate offers on our land any day now right, huh, Millie?"

I roll my eyes at her usual comment and open my mouth to respond before Miss Ethel steps in. "Oh, you old hag, would you give it up already? This town is lucky to have Millie, and if you could step out of your Hallmark fantasy world you would see that she's not here to take our land. Now, I swear to God, if you run this sweet girl off, I'll make sure you're never invited to the monthly bridge luncheons ever again."

Brian and I make eye contact, and I have to look away to keep from bursting into laughter. Miss Sally makes a face at Ethel before rolling her eyes. "Sure, y'all just don't come crying to me when it turns out I was right." With that, she turns and makes her way toward the door.

"Miss Ethel, I don't think I've ever been more in the Christmas spirit after that," Brian says, causing all of us to chuckle.

"Oh dear, she's not usually that bad, but you know how she gets about newcomers. Don't worry, hun, she'll get over it. But until then, if you need anyone to give her a good talkin' to, you just let me know."

I smile, touched by her show of support for me. I lean over and wrap my arm around the older woman. "Thank you, Miss Ethel. I'll keep you updated."

"You do that. Well, we're gonna go grab some drinks, but next time you're on your run, just stop by. I'm always up, and I would love to chat with you over some muffins," she says, before moving further into the room.

I'm still not convinced she's not working for a secret government agency, but I have to admit the older woman has grown on me over the last few weeks.

Brian and I continue mingling with the guests as they make their way inside, until everyone's arrived. We take a moment, watching everyone dancing, enjoying the hors d'oeuvres and the wine, and chatting. I feel a swell of pride in my chest because I did this. After taking in the room, he turns to and says, "God, I love this town. And thank you for making this a reality."

"Of course," I say with a smile. "And I have to agree with you. This town is pretty special."

"Yeah?" he asks, as he waits for me to continue.

"Yeah. You and I both know that I wasn't really sure what I was looking for when I got stranded here, but I have to admit that I think this town has been exactly what I needed."

He smiles, just as the band begins to play a rendition of "Winter Wonderland" and Brian holds out his hand to me. "Feel like dancing?" he asks.

"Sure," I say with a smile, rising from my seat and taking his hand. He pulls me close, and we begin swaying to the music.

"Well, Millie, I have to admit, I agree with you. I think Springside looks good on you," he teases, and I smile. But at the same time, his words remind me that technically after tonight, I'm not quite sure where we stand. I go back and forth, wanting to enjoy the moment but suddenly feeling like I won't be able to relax until I know exactly what he's thinking.

"Uhh, Brian," I say quietly as we sway to the music. "Can I ask you something?"

"Sure, Mills. You already know you can," he replies, and I don't miss the concern in his voice at my tone.

"Do you want me to stay?" I ask, feeling my heart start to race in my chest as I wait for his response.

He looks at me dumbfounded and I have to fight the urge to lean in and kiss the crinkle on his brow. "What?" he asks.

"After tonight, the Christmas events are done," I say, my stomach churning in knots about how he might respond. "So, do you want me to stay?

"What?" Brian says again, not moving and looking at me in confusion.

"I mean…do you want me to stay in Springside?" I blurt, unable to hold it in any longer.

Well, shit, I guess either way, I'm about to get my answer.

CHAPTER 19
BRIAN

"I mean…do you want me to stay in Springside?"

I hear the question, but it takes my brain a moment to catch up. Instead, I stare at her dumbfounded, before I register the hesitant look on her face.

My God, I'm an idiot. I've spent the last month consumed by this beautiful creature in front of me, but I've never been direct about what I want after tonight, scared I'd run her off. And now, she's thinking about leaving.

"Mills, I realize I haven't made myself clear. But I think it's my turn to beg. Please stay. Yes, this town has its quirks, but I promise they'll grow on you. Please, be mine. To be honest, I don't think… I just need you to know there's no way I'm letting you leave. Not without a fight. I know this place can be a little too much, and God only knows you're way overqualified for the job here at Deer Valley, but you belong here.

"Also, while we're just putting everything out there, I know you said you didn't want a label right now, and I promise, I get it. And I know it's probably too fast after everything you've been through over the last few weeks. But, Millie Pouncey, I'm completely in love with you," I admit, unable to stop the words from coming out of my mouth.

Her face morphs into shock, and I briefly worry that I've freaked her out, so I rush to say, "You don't have to say anything back. I'm sorry, I—"

"Brian, damn it, would you let me talk?" she interrupts, drawing my attention back to her perfect face. I realize then that her previous shocked expression has turned into a grin that takes up her whole face, and I feel a surge of hope that she might feel the same way I do.

"What I was trying to say," she starts, once she's sure she has my full attention, "is that I love you too. You're right…it's probably a little crazy, but you've filled the last month with more laughter, fun, and love than I've had in the last ten years… So, if you want me…I'll stay, because I'm just as completely in love with you too."

I feel the smile taking over my face and pull her closer to me. She rests her head on my shoulder, and we dance for a moment before I whisper, "There is one thing I feel like I need to confess."

She pulls back and I don't miss the concerned look on her face. "Uhh, okay, what is it?"

"You know all those lattes you've been bringing me?" I ask as we continue to sway to the music.

"Yeah, what about them?" she inquires warily.

"Umm, I actually can't stand the taste of cinnamon. Basically, anything other than vanilla makes me gag. But you were so excited about them, I couldn't make myself tell you to stop bringing them."

I fight the urge to laugh at her expression as she says, "You mean you've been drinking something you can't stand for a month now, just because you wanted to make me happy?"

"Well, yeah, I guess that about sums it up," I tell her with a laugh.

"God, I really do love you," she whispers, and the look of sincerity on her face makes all the cinnamon sips worth it.

After that, I don't think about anything other than the need to kiss her. Ignoring the fact that we're in public with a room full of people who definitely will notice what I'm about to do, I lean down and pull her into me, kissing her hard. Her mouth meets mine, and I fight the urge to groan at how good she always tastes. I run my tongue across her bottom lip, urging her to open for me and deepen the kiss until we're both panting.

As we pull apart, I realize the rest of the room has erupted into cheers. Millie and I look at each other and then out at the crowd of people celebrating like their team just won the Iron Bowl.

"By golly George, it really is a Christmas miracle," Huey hollers, clapping his hands as a huge smile takes over his face.

"It's about damn time," Miss Ethel yells from over by the bar.

"Hell yeah! Pretty sure I won the bet," Miss Agnes cheers.

Millie and I shoot each other confused looks, neither of us really understanding what's going on. "Umm, someone wanna let us in on the good news?" I ask, waiting for someone to let us in on whatever secret we've obviously been left out of.

Everyone in the room looks around at each other, before Huey finally says, "Well, you see there may have been a little bit of meddling going on behind the scenes."

"May have been?" I question as Huey glances down, unable to meet my gaze.

"All right, fine. Everyone in this room is guilty of being a nosey son of a bitch," he admits.

Millie and I look at each other before both erupting into laughter. "No shit, Sherlock. So, go ahead and admit whatever it is you've done," I command.

"Well, we might have meddled a bit, okay? We just saw immediately how good you and Millie would be together, so we made sure y'all had an opportunity to really get to know each other," Huey says, still refusing to make eye contact with either of us.

"Okayyyyy… How exactly did y'all manage that?" I ask, ready for him to spit it out.

"Ugh, y'all the gig's up. Plus, it looks like it worked anyway.

We might as well tell him what we did," Bridget says, stepping out of the crowd.

"Thank God," I murmur under my breath, waiting for her to continue.

"So, basically everything we've told y'all since Millie got into town is a complete lie… All those nights that you were supposed to have help, or the lights went out, or Huey had to run, or for an emergency, or whatever… We set all of that up to make sure y'all had to spend time together," she admits proudly.

"I knew it," I yell, shaking my head. "Stomach bug, my ass. And every time we couldn't get anyone to answer the phone…"

Millie just laughs, thinking about all the "accidents" we've seen over the last few weeks before gasping. "Wait… My room… There's no way…"

My eyes widen, looking at Bridget who grins. "Guilty…"

I groan. "Bridget, do you know how many times I've called the insurance company and the contractors… I wondered why you kept insisting that I didn't need to go in there…"

She lets out a laugh before saying, "Relax, Brian. John with insurance and the contractors were all in on it too. And don't pretend that y'all being roommates didn't have its advantages."

Millie and I shake our heads again at her comment before Millie says, "Y'all are too much. Wait…what if we really couldn't stand each other, or I got freaked out, or…"

"Uhh, and this was where I came in." I hear a voice say, causing Millie to look around frantically for the source. *Wait… Is that who I think it is… There's no way…*

"Is that…" Millie says, continuing to look around at the faces in the crowd.

"Here, sis," Lizzie's voice calls and Bridget holds the phone up in front of her face where she's FaceTiming my sister. "Damn, I really wish I was seeing that expression in person."

With this latest twist, we're officially speechless, so Millie just stammers. "Wh-wh-what? How? I don't…"

"Well, you listed me as your emergency contact when you

filled out your employee paperwork that first night, and after Bridget and Huey talked, they realized that y'all could be really good together. But we all knew it would take months for y'all to make the moves… So, they called me to see what I thought about doing a little matchmaking under the mistletoe."

Millie's no longer able to stop the laughter that has been building since her sister started her explanation, bursting into a fit of giggles. "Oh my word, you are such a traitor," she accuses.

"Meh, don't even pretend that you weren't into him, sis." Lizzie shrugs through the camera. "My job was to call Bridget if you started to get freaked out or if you didn't seem too into him. If I did, she was going to claim that the room was fixed, and all our antics would stop. But we both know that didn't happen…"

"And what about me?" I ask, not because I'm angry but more because I'm curious what their plan was.

"Uhh, sorry bro," Will calls out sheepishly. "You know I usually stay out of stuff like this, but Caroline and the girls roped me in. When I showed up the other night, it was to see if their plan was working. If not, I was supposed to text Huey, and more of the volunteers would have shown up. But again…we both know how that went."

It's clear neither of us know what to say, because we stare at the room in shock for a few more minutes. Finally, I shake my head and admit. "This is not what I was expecting, and like you said, I can't be too upset with the outcome. But did anyone ever tell you that y'all are the noisiest group of people I've ever met? Like seriously, y'all have a problem."

The room erupts into laughter at that, with several of the ladies nodding and giggling at my statement. Several of the locals start to make their way toward us, either to congratulate us or pester us for details, but before they get too close, I lean down and whisper in Millie's ear. "Are you ready to get out of here? The band is finishing up, and if we don't leave now, we'll never get away from 'em."

"Brian, we can't just leave! What about the clean up?" she

asks, clearly already dreading the couple of hours it will probably take for us to get everything put away.

"Bridget can shut it down. Pretty sure it's the least she can do after everything she pulled the last few weeks," I growl, making her laugh before adding, "Plus, if I don't get inside you soon, I'm gonna lose my fucking mind."

"Let's go," she whispers, just as Miss Sally and Miss Ethel come closer. I try not to let my face show my impatience as they start asking questions, but our earlier confession has me completely focused on getting out of here as quickly as possible.

"Well girl, I reckon I was wrong about you," Miss Sally admits begrudgingly to Millie. "But you just know, I ain't letting my guard down completely yet."

I don't miss the look of mistrust on her face while Millie and I fight the urge to laugh at her antics. "Yes ma'am," she says with a smile.

"Honey, I need to know all the details...when did all this happen?" Miss Ethel asks. "You know I've been suspicious for the last few weeks, but Huey and Bridget refused to tell us much, I—"

"Oh well...actually, I'm so sorry, Miss Ethel, but we've gotta go," I interrupt. "I promise Millie will talk to you soon!" I call over my shoulder as Millie grabs my hand and we make our run for the exit.

CHAPTER 20

MILLIE

"Brian, I swear to all things holy, if you don't get us home, I'm gonna lose my mind," I growl, leaning over the console and teasing the front of his pants with my hand once we finally get in the truck.

He presses down harder on the accelerator, and I feel the truck lurch with the increased speed. The gala was wonderful, but after everything, I'm desperate to have him inside me. Deciding to tease him some, I untuck his shirt and slide my hand under his belt to run my hand along his waist, before finally unbuckling his belt and running my fingers up and down his boxer-covered shaft. I smile when I feel him tense, and he jerks the wheel.

"Fuck, Mills, if you don't stop, I'm gonna run over Miss Ethel's mailbox. Do you really want to explain that one to her?"

I give him a look, feigning innocence before leaning down and pulling his boxers down to take him into my mouth.

"Jesus," he growls, flexing his hips and pushing himself a little deeper. "Damn, Mills, if you keep this up, I'm not gonna make it home. Feeling your sweet little mouth wrapped around my cock for the first time is one of the hottest things I've ever seen."

I let out a little moan at his praise, bobbing up and down and flicking out my tongue across his tip. He growls, and I feel him gripping the steering wheel tighter, trying to get us home. I've never enjoyed giving head before, but as I tease Brian, I see its appeal for the first time. I'm already riding such a high from hearing him say he loves me and the relief of the gala going smoothly, but the way he swells in my mouth each time I run my tongue down his dick is addictive.

I continue teasing him until we pull into the driveway a few minutes later. He's barely thrown the truck in park before he tucks himself back into his pants and opens the door. He jumps out and leans back in, dragging me across the front seat.

"God, you're driving me fucking crazy," he murmurs before threading his hands under my legs and picking me up. He slams the truck door closed and carries me to the house, bridal style. "All I wanted was to pull you in my lap and fuck you in the driveway, but I fear the STS may never survive that type of gossip. So, I'm gonna get us inside before I rip this dress off and fuck you against the wall."

"Yes, sir," I whisper, knowing that the phrase drives him wild. Sure enough, he lets out a growl as he fumbles for his house key. As soon as we're in the door, he's on me, unzipping my dress and dragging it down my body until I'm naked in front of him except for my red lace thong.

"Hell, Millie, you're gorgeous," he marvels, pulling back and admiring my lingerie in the glow of the Christmas lights from the tree across the room. After a moment, he reaches up and rips my panties at the hip. "But as much as I like these on you, they gotta go." As soon as I'm completely bare, he sinks to his knees and throws one of my legs around his neck. He attacks my pussy with his mouth, licking and sucking, and I have to admit I'm grateful for the wall behind me holding me up.

"Ahh, Brian, don't stop," I beg as he thrusts two fingers into me at the same time he nips at my clit with his teeth. *Damn, how the hell does he even do that.* Each time he touches me, I think it can't get better, and each time, he's proven me wrong, I've never come as hard in my life as I do when he fucks me or teases me with his tongue. "I'm close."

"Good, but when you come, it's gonna be on my dick," he insists, pulling back and rising to his full height. Grabbing my hand, he pulls me behind him until we're behind the couch that faces the tree. He drops a few kisses on my lips before he wraps his hand around my throat the way I like and turns me toward the tree. My back is to him and he uses his hand to push me down until I'm laying over the back of the couch. Once he's satisfied with my position, he undoes his pants, dropping them down and grabbing my hips. I feel his cock bump my entrance before he rocks into me with one swift motion. "Shit, so good."

"Uh-huh," I murmur as he stills. I try to shift my hips to get some traction, but the way he has me between his hard body and the couch makes it impossible to move.

"Hmm, looks like you're in quite the position," he teases before continuing. "If you want me to move so you can come, you're gonna have to beg."

I try to hide the fact that I'm halfway between groaning and smiling at his words. I've learned over the last few days that he still loves when I ask for what I want, both in and out of the bedroom. And normally, I enjoy the games we play, but tonight, I just want him inside me as quickly as possible. "Please, please, let me come."

"That's my girl," he growls, pulling out and starting to push back inside, slowly at first. He gets a little faster with each thrust, and it only takes a few moments before I let out another moan, wiggling my hips as much as I can to get some friction against my clit.

Brian immediately realizes what I need, reaching his hand between us and thrumming his fingers against me. "You know I love playing with you like this," he admits. "You're always so fucking wet and ready for me."

I'm so lost to how incredible he's making me feel that I can't respond, letting out a high-pitched scream as he fucks me through my orgasm. "That's right baby, come for me," he growls. "You know how much I love feeling your pussy clench around me."

As soon as he says the words, he pushes into me harder, making the orgasm rolling through me keep going. His fingers flex with his grip on my hips as I feel warm spurts of his cum hitting my inner walls. God, the feeling of him claiming me in such a primal way never gets old.

He leans down after a moment, pressing his front to my back and kissing me before pulling out and reaching down to pick me up again.

"Come on, let's get cleaned up," he says, and I just nod, immediately feeling exhausted after the chaos of the last few days.

He carries me into the bathroom, placing me on my feet beside the shower as he fiddles with the controls to get the water temperature right. He's taken to washing my hair before he bathes me over the last two nights, and I'm already imagining how good his hands will feel on me under the steam of the hot shower. Neither of us say anything as we shower, both of us tired but content with the silence.

After showering and standing under the hot water for several minutes, he reaches out and hands me a towel before grabbing one for himself. We dry ourselves off and step out of the shower, before going through our nighttime routine. As soon as my teeth are brushed and my face is clean, Brian walks over from where he was leaning against the counter watching me. As he picks me up again and carries me to the bedroom, I tell him, "You know, I really could walk."

"I know, but then I wouldn't get to be this close to you," he says with a grin.

"Well, you've got me there," I tell him with a laugh, nuzzling my head into the crook of his neck. When we get to the bed, he manages to maneuver me so that I stay in his arms, and he leans down to pull the covers over us.

As we get settled into bed, I look over and see the clock sitting on the bedside table. It's well after midnight, so it's officially Christmas morning.

"Dang, I bet we'll miss our visit from Santa this year since we weren't at home in time," I tease, and Brian lets out a laugh.

"I hate to break it to you, Mills, but I'm pretty sure after the number of times we've fucked the last few days we were on the 'naughty list' anyway," he remarks, and I roll my eyes at his joke.

"Hmm, whatever you say. Anyway, all I was trying to say before I was so rudely interrupted," I say with a wink at Brian to let him know I'm teasing, "was Merry Christmas. I never thought I'd say this, but I can't imagine anywhere else in the world I'd want to spend it."

"Merry Christmas, Mills. I'm glad to hear it because like I told you earlier, if you ever decide to leave, I'm not staying here without you," Brian whispers, placing a kiss on my lips and throwing his arm across me to pull me closer to him. "Oh, and in case you forgot, I love you."

"Goodnight, Brian, and in case you didn't know, I love you back," I tell him, curling my body around him. And as I start to drift off to sleep, I can't help but think that this new life I've found over the last month is better than any gift we may find under the tree in the morning.

EPILOGUE

ONE YEAR LATER

MILLIE

"Okay, Mills, you have to keep the blindfold on if you want your surprise," Brian says as he leads me out of the truck.

"Ugh, fine, but I don't understand why you can't just wrap it and put it under a tree like a normal person," I grumble.

It's Christmas morning, and usually I would be feeling holly and jolly, but Brian woke me up before six and told me to get ready for wherever he's taking me. He's well aware by now that waking me before the sun on a day I don't have to go to work would make me a little extra grouchy, but here we are. After getting dressed, he told me to get in the car and he blindfolded me while we drove for a few minutes.

"You know, if you've been a serial killer this whole time and you're just deciding to act on it, I'm gonna be really freaking pissed," I tease as we walk for a few minutes longer.

"Nope, not a serial killer, just a guy trying to surprise his girl-friend for Christmas," he replies.

"Ugh okay, I'm sure whatever it is, is incredible, but in case you forgot, we didn't get home until almost one this morning.

What do ya know, apparently the gala lasts way longer if you don't sneak off an hour in to have sex," I joke, and I hear Brian chuckle.

"Okay, okay, I admit that the few hours of sleep is less than ideal, but I promise, I think this surprise is worth it," he says, before slowing me to a stop. "All right, we're here. Are you ready?"

"Yeah, can I take the blindfold off?" I ask, reaching up and touching the silk on my face.

"Almost, give me just one second… Okay, whenever you're ready," he says, and I tear the tie off my face, anxious to see what he's made such a big deal over.

"Oh," I say, as soon as I open my eyes, and immediately I pause, unable to make any sense of what I'm seeing.

We're at Coopers' Tree Farm, but the maze looks completely different than it did last week when we left after the Mistletoe Maze. The lights and trees are the same, but the clearing is covered with fake snow and there's tons of pink and green ornaments all over the closest trees. Mixed in with the ornaments are pictures of Brian and I over the last year, and the sun is rising just above the tops of the trees, casting everything in a pinkish-orange light. I look over to say something to Brian, and it finally registers that he's down on one knee.

"Millie Pouncey, it's been over a year since that freak snowstorm all but dumped you on my doorstep and woke me up to everything I was missing. I was basically sleepwalking through life, but you made me realize that it's not selfish to want someone who makes me as happy as you make me. And, while we probably won't have snow like that for another decade or two, I'm hoping this time, instead of bringing us together, this snow will help keep us together. That it'll make you decide to take my last name and be mine forever. Because in case you haven't noticed, I'm madly in love with you, and nothing would make me happier than you agreeing to be my wife."

I stare at him in shock for a few more seconds before pulling him up and kissing him hard. "Oh my God, are you serious?" I ask between kisses.

"Uhh, yeah," he says nervously. "I mean, if you need to think about it I totally under—" he starts, and I realize I never actually answered him out loud.

"Oh, God, yes, Brian, absolutely. You really want me to be your wife?" I ask, feeling some of my old insecurities starting to sneak in.

"Uhh, duh," he says, like that's the silliest question he's ever heard.

"You know I'm kinda 0-1 in that area, right?" I tease, trying to disguise how nervous I'm feeling. I haven't given a single thought to my ex-husband in several months, but Brian's proposal has a lot of those old feelings floating to the surface.

"Bullshit, Mills. I'm sorry, but you and I both know that isn't true. I've never been as happy as I am with you," he admits, and I can't resist the urge to kiss him.

"Me either," I tell him honestly. It's true. The last year has been nothing short of incredible. I've organized over thirty weddings along with countless birthday parties, office dinners, and other various functions. Brian swears he's never seen Deer Valley as busy as it has been, and I feel a little swell of pride every time he makes that statement. On top of that, Bridget and I have become great friends, and Brian and I have continued to live together. I offered to get an apartment after I got my settlement from the divorce, but he refused to hear a word of it. Some days he comes to Deer Valley with me, and others he goes to City Hall for the day and meets me back at the inn when he's finished. But either way, we spend each night at home, cuddling under the covers, kissing, and learning more about each other.

"Oh my God, we're getting married," I squeal, as it hits me that he actually wants to spend the rest of his life with me.

"Damn right, we are," he says before adding, "Good thing I know a pretty incredible wedding planner, huh?"

I laugh at his comment, before pulling him to me and kissing him hard. I'm wishing this kiss could go further and that we were back in the privacy of his truck already when I hear some shuffling in the trees. I look over to see Bridget and Lizzie jumping out from wherever they were hiding, and I'm pretty sure the screech I let out can be heard in Saddle Ridge. But really, I can't help it.

My sister and I have made plans four different times over the last year, but between our busy schedules and everything else we've had going on, we've had to stick to weekly phone dates and occasional FaceTime calls. I did make it to New York for Fashion Week to see her first show, but she was so slammed with work, I didn't get to spend any time with her.

"Oh my God, what the hell are you doing here?" I ask, still in shock that she's actually here.

"I'm sorry, sis, but did you really think I would miss this?" she responds, pulling me into a hug. "Damn, I'm so happy for you. I've missed you so much."

"Wait," Bridget says, glancing around at the group of us. "I think I'm missing something… Where the hell's the ring?"

Lizzie and I both freeze, as Brian shakes his head. "Damn it, y'all came in before I could give it to her. I told you to wait until I was done."

"Umm, first of all, who the hell doesn't do the ring with the whole down on one knee thing? And second of all, I was pretty sure y'all were about to go at it right here if we didn't interrupt you, and I love you both, but that's pretty much the last thing I want to see," Bridget retorts.

"Shit, I knew I shouldn't have told you when I was planning to do this. You can be such a—" Brian groans, until Lizzie interrupts him.

"Both of you, shut the heck up. Let's see the damn ring," she yells, and I can't help but laugh.

Some would probably be annoyed at the chaos of this proposal, but I can't imagine anything more perfect. But Brian proves me wrong when he pulls out the most perfect ring I've ever seen in my life. The gold band covered in diamonds that start small get bigger the closer they get to the huge teardrop shaped stone in the center. He slips it on my finger, and I'm not surprised when it fits perfectly.

"How the hell did you pull all this off?" I ask, blinking back the tears of happiness that are currently threatening to run down my face.

"Well, let's see. I got Lizzie's number off your phone, and I asked her if she wanted to surprise you," he starts before my sister interrupts him again.

"Which obviously I did," she whispers, grabbing my hand and inspecting my new ring.

"Right," Brian says, before continuing. "Then, I asked Huey to get here around four this morning and keep an eye on the snow machines… Speaking of which, he should be…"

"I'm here!" he calls, coming out from another spot in the tree. "I was trying to follow directions and make sure you were actually done before I came out."

"Hey, that's not fair," Bridget starts, but the look Brian sends her makes her fall silent.

"Anyway, I hear congratulations are in order," Huey says with a smile. "Well, let me see the dang thing."

"Oh, right," I say, holding out my hand for him to examine before he pulls me into a tight hug.

"I don't know what it was about that day you wrecked in front of my house, Miss Millie, but remember how I told you this town might just have what you needed? Well, I think it's safe to say you found it," Huey whispers under his breath so that the two of us are the only ones that can hear, and I feel my eyes fill with tears again.

"I think you're right, Huey," I tell him, before Brian pulls me back into his arms.

"Anyway, like I was saying," he says, glaring at the group in front of us, silently threatening them not to interrupt him again. "Huey set up the snow, and Bridget and your sister decorated the trees. I'm sorry it's still early, but I wanted to be here at sunrise. Plus, I figured you'd want to squeeze in as much time with your sister as you could."

"God, I love you," I tell him, leaning in to kiss him.

"All right, you lovebirds, that's enough of that," Lizzie teases, snapping a few pictures of us. "All right, I'm freezing. Are y'all ready?"

"To go where?" I ask. "Y'all are welcome at the house, but I don't think I have much to offer in the form of snacks."

"Did you really think we'd expect you to feed us to celebrate your engagement? We have a few things at Deer Valley, so we'll meet you over there," Bridget says, and the three of them leave so that Brian and I are alone again.

"You know, I can't wait to marry you. And I should have known after the way you came into my life that the rest of my days would never be boring," he teases, pulling me to him and wrapping his arms around me before kissing my neck. "God, I'd give anything to take you home and properly celebrate this engagement, but something tells me those three together will not be the most patient."

I smile at him before looking down at the ring on my finger.

"That's okay. Good thing we've got forever together," I tell him, before grabbing his hand. "Now, what do you say we go start it?"

ACKNOWLEDGMENTS

Wow! I can't believe y'all are finally holding another one of my books in your hands! If you've followed along on socials, you know this year has been a bit rough in my personal life. There were times I was convinced I'd never get to publish another book, but here we are. My incredible support system pushed me to help make this became a reality, and I'm so grateful!

First of all, the only reason this was possible is the support of my sweet hubby. C, I love you endlessly. I couldn't do any of this without you, and every time you encourage me to go after my dreams, I fall a little more in love with you. This year has been a roller coaster for us, but you've never wavered in your support. I know making these books a reality often means a lot of takeout and piles of laundry, but you never complain, and I couldn't love you more.

To my Mom, Dad, Nonnie, and Dah, thank you for always being my biggest hype team. You're still not allowed to read them, but I love your enthusiasm for these stories. You've always pushed me to be go after the things that make me happy, and love you all always!

Brittni, what on earth would I do without you?! Thank you for sorting through my chaos and helping me bring this story to life! Your patience with me and your incredible feedback both mean the world to me! Thank you for being the best editor and friend!

Caroline, Emma, and Erica, y'all are rockstars! Y'all are the best editors and proofreaders a girl could ask for, and I'm so grateful for each of you! Thank y'all so much for all the grammar and comma help! I adore working with all of you!

To my betas— Emily, Hunter, Emma, Brianna, and Morgan— reading y'all's unhinged comments and feedback brought me so much joy, and I can't thank y'all enough for helping me make this story what is is!

Ali, you already know I adore you! Thank you for always making all my graphic and cover dreams come true!

Maren and Bianca, pretty sure this book would still be missing the last 10k without y'all! Thanks for sprinting with me!

To my author besties Alexis, Ambar, Jenn— I hope you know how invaluable y'all's support and encouragement is to me! Thanks for answering all my silly questions and being such great cheerleaders!

To my ARC team and the rest of the Bookstagram community, thank you so much for hyping me up even when I had to take a step back for a few months. Y'all's DMs make my day, and I can't thank you enough for every share, post, and tag.

And finally, sweet reader, thank you for taking a chance on Brian and Millie's story! None of this is possible without you, so thank you so much for your support!

LIST OF CONTENT WARNINGS

Explicit Sexual Content
Mentions of Divorce
Parental Loss (Off Page)

ABOUT THE AUTHOR

Hollie Luckie is a small town girl that wholeheartedly believes in happily ever afters. Between teaching and writing romance, she is always getting lost in a fictional world. She resides in Alabama with her high school sweetheart, her dog, and her own farm of quirky farm animals. You can find Hollie on Instagram at @authorhollieluckie or on Goodreads.